Project Paris

•

The fashion-forward
adventures of Imogene

Written by
Lisa Barham

Illustrated by
Sujean Rim

SIMON PULSE

New York   London   Toronto   Sydney

Project Paris

The fashion-forward
adventures of Imogene

For Tom and Jack, with love

SIMON PULSE ✳ An imprint of Simon & Schuster Children's Publishing Division ✳ 1230 Avenue of the Americas, New York, NY 10020 ✳ Copyright © 2007 by Lisa Barham ✳ Illustrations copyright © 2007 by Sujean Rim ✳ All rights reserved, including the right of reproduction in whole or in part in any form. ✳ SIMON PULSE and colophon are registered trademarks of Simon & Schuster, Inc. ✳ Designed by Karin Paprocki ✳ The text of this book was set in Cochin. ✳ Manufactured in the United States of America ✳ First Simon Pulse edition June 2007 ✳
10 9 8 7 6 5 4 3 2 1
Library of Congress Control Number 2006940711
ISBN-13: 978-1-4169-1444-0 ✳ ISBN-10: 1-4169-1444-7

acknowledgments

I sincerely wish to thank my editor, the wonderful Bethany Buck. Thank you Jen Bergstrom, Caroline Abbey, Orly Sigal, Lila Haber, Paul Crighton, Lucille Rettino, Karin Paprocki, and everyone at Simon & Schuster. A huge thank-you to Sujean Rim, to whom I am indebted for her beautiful artwork. Thank you to my fantastic agent, Jodi Reamer.

To Suzanne Hoover and my writers group: Lucy Hedrick, Weezie Mackey, Alex McNab, Cathy Sibirzeff, Megan Harris, and Lyn Harmon—I thank you all for your patience and encouragement. Thank you, Frank Spina, for your friendship and guidance, and my sister, Paula, for a lifetime of fashion inspiration.

Last but never least, I thank my family—this book would never have been written without the complete support and scrupulous eye of my husband, Tom, and my loving son, Jack.

About Moi

Name: Imogene

Age: 17

Status: N/A

Hometown: Greenwich, CT (that's gren-itch, not green-witch — duh!)

Body type: All arms & legs

Zodiac sign: Aries

Member since: Yesterday

School: Greenwich Country Academy (GCA for short)

Accomplishments: President of the GCA Style Council, inventor of the *Imogenius* SoftWear program, founder of the SPFA (Society for the Prevention of Fashion Angst)

Occupation: Culturepreneur (aka fashion forecasting intern)

Interests & Hobbies: Writing my school newspaper's "The Daily Obsession" fashion column, fashion! (duh!), making movies (double duh! That's why they call this a *video* diary), old-style scrapbooking, (I know, it's a tad dorky, so sue me!), my ginormous Hello Kitty collection! I am writing my memoirs (my pen name, should it ever come up, is Melandria Alexandria Angelina Aphrodite).

Where I'll Be This Summer: Hint No. 1: Not in Greenwich. Hint No. 2: *Je veux vivre à Paris!*

Last Log-in: Eight hours ago, pre–35,000 feet above planet Earth

I Heart: Lip gloss, friendship, freebies, positive affirmations, petit fours, Château de Ver-sigh! (a girl can dream, can't she?), Jeffrey, Barneys, a single rose, kisses, hearts, butterflies, and the color pink. I love Jackie O.,

Annie Hall, *Amélie*, and old black-and-white movies—which I generally watch with my BFF, who's a complete nut job for old Hollywood! (She even names her dresses after old film stars—I'm currently praying there's a Marilyn or a Judy in my future.)

𝒥 *Skull & Crossbones*: Missed sample sales, style stealers, broken dreams, deadlines, phony peeps, the gloomies, and *le coif de* "The Donald."

Today's Affirmation: I live my higher purpose: I wear couture!

chapter one

Lost in Translation

date: JUNE 18
daily obsession: FRECKLES

I am extremely disappointed in the utter lack of freckles on girls today. Therefore, I have taken it upon myself to single-handedly bring them back.

✳   ✳   ✳

N o sooner had I attached his leash than he was off like a shot, dragging me and my hastily collected belongings into the aisle with him. I tossed my iPhone into my bag, hit the record button on my camcorder, and held on for dear life.

"Toy, Toy!" I shouted. There's nothing worse than being involuntarily pulled along by a frantic French bulldog [fashion phylum: *canis misbehavous*] on a short leash and getting dirty looks from the irritated passengers who were unintentionally knocked back into their seats.

"Toy," I pleaded, "mind your manners!"

But Toy paid no attention. It was no use trying to reason with him. He just kept barking and pushing forward. Passengers and flight attendants leapt out of the way, protesting vehemently. Others who weren't so lucky had their heads, butts, and legs thwacked by my overstuffed bag.

This wasn't exactly how I had pictured my arrival. My plan was to record for posterity, *and* for my school summer intern project, my historic landing on French soil. I was specially dressed for the event, festooned in a vintage pink maribou feathered head pouf, a pale pink sunburst pleated gossamer-light fairy tale of a dress, and vintage (as in last year's) gold platforms. Unfortunately, the look that I'd planned, primped, and perfected was now more than a tad askew.

"You can't shove your way out of the plane! Wait your turn!" an angry passenger shouted.

"I'm not shoving. He is!" I said, pointing to Toy.

The cabin door swung open and we bolted past the angry Christian Lacroix–adorned flight attendants.

Without time for so much as a good-bye or a thank-you, Toy pulled me onto the breezeway. Packages, angry passengers, and the flight attendants trailed in our wake.

My arm was stretched like a rubber band as I struggled desperately to hang on to his leash. "Slow down, boy!" Although who could blame him? I could barely tolerate seven and a half hours of nonstop boredom, aka plane travel. At least I had my video diary to update, and my to-do lists, and my can't-live-without lists, and plans to make, and people to talk to, and society to break into. I mean, *he* was only a dog.

We flew down the breezeway. I tried repositioning the carry-on now sliding down my shoulder, while juggling bags, several magazines, and a cup of jet-lag remedy. Normally this type of multitasking didn't pose a problem, but I guess with all the excitement, I was a smidge off my game.

We were weaving in and out of the crowd of passengers, when suddenly the inevitable happened. Without warning, my right foot decided to stop moving without bothering to inform the rest of my body.

FUMFFFFFFFFFFF!!!!!

A loop in the worn-down indoor-outdoor carpet seemed to have caught one of my heels, sending me tumbling across the carpet. Everything—including my Smythson journal, the magazines, the jet-lag remedy, my camcorder, and half a dozen petit fours (not to mention my flip-flopping internal organs)—flew through the air like a troupe of rogue Wallendas.

Mental summer vow: When with Toy, enlist ballet flats whenever possible (at the very least kitten heels!).

Everything was ruined. My video diary, my clothing, and my ego. I lay there helplessly, praying that this wasn't an omen of things to come. The memory of last summer's shoe fiasco still sent shivers down my spine.

Toy, by now, had bolted through the crowd—his loose leash tripping many unsuspecting travelers, more than a few of whom glared at me before limping off. I chose to ignore them. I mean, I absolutely refuse to begin my summer with a case of the gloomies, especially on the eve of my new life *à la Parisienne* because, as everyone knows, it's no longer fashionable for *Parisiennes* to be depressed. And if there's one thing you can say about me, it's that I'm fashionable.

Though I admit it, this debacle was all my fault. I mean, I completely ignored e-mail etiquette rule No. 22: IM-ing BFF while debarking from airplanes in four-inch heels while recording historic entrée into Paris via video diary could have catastrophic consequences.

With a deep sigh, I collected my scattered belongings, tossing everything back into my Dolce Miss Perfect bag, including my journal. It's a requirement, you know. Last year's journal, I could have written a book from. Though I am not by any stretch of the imagination a Jane Austen, I am, as part of my school's summer intern program, required to set pen to paper in order to present a full accounting of my summer experiences. This summer, not only will I be writing about and forecasting fashion trends, I shall write about all the glorious things I experience in life and record it all for prosperity (and a few extra credit points). Which I imagine will be too numerous to mention.

Eventually I found Toy making friends with another French bulldog. She was all white and wore a sweet pink ribbon leash. It was attached to an owner, who was seemingly unaware of the melee that had just occurred.

I *had* thought about leaving Toy behind, but aside from visiting the home of our ancestors and getting some much-needed cultural diversity, I just couldn't bear the thought of being without him an entire summer. (Not only that, he secretly finds my parents a tad boring.)

"So it's you he was after!" I said to the object of Toy's affections.

Toy just gazed up at me with the biggest you-know-what-eating grin on his face. (Yes, he smiles. Don't all dogs?) Despite the fact that I was beyond frazzled, not to mention more than a hair disheveled, I reached into my bag and pulled out his favorite toy.

"You are such a bad boy!" I said to him. "You know you don't deserve this, don't you?" I couldn't help smiling when he bit into Sock Monkey and offered it up to his new would-be girlfriend.

"That's enough of that," I said, picking him up securely.

He whimpered.

"And don't think you're going to get away with that sort of behavior this summer. I'll talk to you privately about that later."

Mental note: Check out puppy charm schools toute de suite!

Not taking any more chances, I wrapped Toy in the snuggly, just-skoshed Air France blanket and proceeded toward baggage claim.

By the time I arrived at the baggage carousels, I was beginning to feel a tad out of sorts. After seven and a half hours of wailing babies, boyfriend broodings, grueling turbulence (so much for flying the friendly skies), and disobedient pets, my fragile state of being and I would rather eat our own eyelashes than go through the final gauntlet of baggage, customs, and human traffic jams.

Thankfully, my luggage was easily found. As was a trolley.

After navigating an *endless* maze of corridors, I entered an enormous room, wall-to-wall with what could only be described as a massive gaggle of humanity. This would be customs, as in extremely long lines, extremely long wait times, and extremely unhappy me. I took a deep breath, resolved myself to fate, and got into line.

Suffice it to say that if this were any other time, I'd have been passing out all over the place, but for the thought that I would soon be reunited with Evie, aka BFF. Evie had been staying with her parents this past week. They had a suite at the Plaza Athénée (five stars of French hotel luxury on Avenue Montaigne), which just so happened to be a hop, skip, and jump away from my other BFFs: Giorgio, Miu Miu, Christian, and Valentino!

Ever since Evie's collection debuted in Hautelaw's "What's Haute" forecast issue last summer, she'd been hotter than hot. Not being one to let her newfound celebrity go to waste, she had immediately applied for a summer internship with every couturier and fashion designer on the planet. It wasn't long before she landed one, at Crispin Lamour—in Paris!! (I swore I'd never submit to BFF envy, but no one saw this one coming.) Crispin Lamour was the top of the heap as far as fashion designers go. Fashion groupies flocked to him at the drop of a red-carpet event. I mean, working as a summer intern at the House of Lamour would undoubtedly fast-forward her aspirations of becoming a real designer someday.

As for me, I couldn't very well leave Evie stranded in a foreign land all alone. What kind of friend would I be? Though there was one teeny little problem: Spring Sommer, (fashion phylum: *Les Trois Coquettes*, subphylum: *Flakus Maximus*) my boss and the owner of Hautelaw.

You see, I had already *promised* her I'd intern again this year. And since I really, really, *reallllly* wanted to do that, Evie and I conspired to kill two birds with one stone (not that I would ever kill any living thing, I mean, I *j'adore* all animals — even iguanas) by making her realize how desperately Hautelaw needed a trend spotter (that would be me) to cover the latest and greatest on the streets of Paris for the next three months. I would also point out that her fiercely despised archrival, Winter Tan, would most certainly be covering Couture Week and would, no doubt, send her new point girl — former Hautelaw traitor and all-around witch-of-the-month hall-of-famer, Brooke (fashion phylum: *The Wolfe Pack*) to do her dirty work.

So I braced myself. Ready to debate, cajole, and otherwise persuade my boss (in her best interests, of course) to speed me off to Paris on the first available flight. As it turned out, instead of encountering resistance, my plan was not only embraced, but I was hailed as a veritable mind reader. You see, Spring had been sitting on some property in the heart of

Paris for several years—part of a settlement from her third or fifth (she could never remember) husband—she decided it was time to put it to good use, jumping at the opportunity to have her intern (in addition to performing my other duties) do all the legwork. Far be it for me to turn down an Eiffel Tower view on the Seine.

Best of all, Evie and I would be living at my Aunt Tamara's, which is to say *practically* on our own. I say *practically* because my parents, in cooperation with Evie's parents, made sure that Mom's sister, *my* Aunt Tamara, who was, as my mother put it, "God knows where half the time," had arranged for "responsible supervision on the premises 24/7." Said supervision was to take the form of a being by the name of Leslie who, according to reliable sources, has been a fixture at Tamara's place for over a year now and more than satisfied the above requirements. Knowing Aunt Tamara, Leslie would likely prove to be a somewhat elderly and demure housekeeper who had long ago given up trying to keep tabs on Tamara's whereabouts and would, like as not, apply the same lack of interest to us. That is, of course, if I made it through customs before my eighteenth birthday.

Other than that, everything was great. Though the buildup to summer began with an unfortunate event involving my love life. As in, Paolo and I broke up. Sort of. He's spending his summer in Italy with his family, so we're kind of taking a little time-out from each other. How did I feel about this? Well, that remains to be seen. I mean, one thing's for sure, I'm putting a lot of energy into trying to put Paolo out of my mind. And spending a summer in Paris was one surefire way to do that. Truth be known, I'm a closet sun worshipper, but due to my extenuating circumstances this summer I've opted to trade in the Long Island Sound—so getting tired—for urban living in a new milieu altogether.

Just like D'Artagnan, the famous Musketeer, who set off for Paris to make his fortune with nothing more than a few simple possessions and the blessings of his father. Though *my* father (*and* my mother) were slightly apprehensive about sending me—their only child—to a foreign country for an entire summer, Aunt Tamara reassured her that it would be the best experience I could ever wish for. After all, *they* did it when they were my age. Mom returned to the States, but Aunt Tamara stayed, never to return. Which, come to think of it, was probably what Mom was worried about.

When I finally wheeled up to the customs station, I expected to breeze right through, having had the foresight to send my summer wardrobe ahead, bringing a set of practically empty (not to mention *totally chic*) Jeremy Scott luggage, thanks to a sudden cash windfall (we'll get to that shortly).

I checked my bag one more time for the required documentation: passport, traveler's checks, car insurance certificate, American driver's license, AmEx card, Toy's vaccination history and certificate from his vet, International AAA membership card, emergency phone numbers and addresses, Première Vision press pass, and most important—couture invitations! Not to mention my iPhone, quad-band chip, camcorder, and digital camera. Yup. All here.

"Avez-vous quelque chose à déclarer?" quipped Customs Agent

Number One, a tall man with a high forehead and large gray eyes. His associate, Customs Agent Number Two (short, pinched face, nose hair), was busy ogling Toy's papers. Toy was busy standing on the counter being Toy.

"Declare? *Moi*?" I chuckled. Part of my summer fantasy was to come to France and enchant the populace with my fluent command of the language. Here was the perfect opportunity to demonstrate a dazzling display of insouciance, charm, and French.

"Votre postiche est très heureux."

Unfortunately, this only served to shock Agent One into clutching the top of his head and turning a brilliant shade of fuchsia. (I was informed later that I had told him that his toupee was happy.)

"What is the purpose of your trip, *mademoiselle*?" he demanded, adjusting his faux hair.

"Je mange des noix pour ma santé."

"We grow grapes in France. Not nuts."

"Are you quite sure?" I heaved, with a suspicious eye.

He glared at me, then proceeded to scrutinize my passport while Agent Two tossed one of my bags on the counter and peered inside.

I cast my gaze around the room and noticed a waiting crowd of people and limo drivers behind glass. Floating above them was my name, MLLE. IMOGENE, scrawled on a wedge of cardboard. The wedge was attached to a large, athletic-looking man wearing mint green Adidas sneakers and matching tracksuit—jacket unzipped just enough to expose a dense forest of chest hair adorned with gold chains by the yard. He was broad but fit, tan, and sported a professional blowout of sandy blond hair à la "The Donald." Double pinky rings, wraparound shades, and a visible scar above his left eyebrow suggested he had had his share of life experience. No doubt a driver sent by Leslie, I mused.

"Your *vêtements, mademoiselle,*" said Agent Two. "They are where?"

"*Vêtements?*"

"Your clothing."

"Ohh, my clothing. Well, I don't have any. I mean, not on me . . . that is, with me. You see, I have this theory about travel . . . because I like to shop. I mean, actually, I *loooooove* to shop. Which is why I *always* travel to foreign countries with empty—"

"*S'il vous plaît, mademoiselle,*" interrupted Agent One impatiently. "Your clothing. It is where?"

"Well, that's what I was trying to tell you. I travel with empty bags so I have lots of room to bring stuff back."

For some reason this occasioned the raising of eyebrows from both agents, at which point they turned away from the counter and engaged in a furtive discussion about what I could only presume was, having glanced in my direction several times, *moi.* Agents One and Two were soon joined by a third. This one had a very large luggage-sniffing German shepherd in tow, who proceeded to sniff Toy.

Needless to say, Toy was *very offended* and nipped the

shepherd's nose, causing him to wail in pain. I immediately snatched up Toy as Agents One through Three spun around and began hollering. Toy fired back with a barrage of yips (mostly directed at Agent One's rug, I couldn't help but notice), while I tried to avoid being eaten by the luggage sniffer. More agents wandered over (along with more luggage sniffers) and joined in the confab. I was in the midst of shouting something in French at Agent Two about civil rights (as it turned out, I was telling him to stuff celery in his underwear), when the man with the MLLE. IMOGENE sign stepped in and spoke to Agent One.

"Got a minute?" he said with a Brooklynese accent.

The two stepped aside for a quick tête-à-tête while the rest of us duked it out at the counter. I watched as the man spoke to Agent One. Shortly thereafter, I was ushered through the gate, where the man with the coif was now waiting.

"That was slick," I said, rolling the trolley forward. "How did you know who I was?"

"I had a feeling," he replied, studying Toy.

"Nice accent, by the way," I said with a smile. "Since when do French limo drivers hail from Brooklyn?"

"You got it all wrong, sweetheart. I'm the guy who's supposed to watch youse all summer."

"What?"

"That's right." He grinned, a gold crown glimmering from somewhere in the recesses of his mouth.

"*You're* Leslie?"

"Yeah, honey. That's me. The one and only."

"But I was expecting a—"

"Woman? I know. Everybody makes that mistake."

"I'm sorry. I didn't mean to offend you or anything."

"Fuhgeddaboudit. I grew up in a tough neighborhood. My mother figured a name like Leslie would keep me on my toes."

"Really? Did it work?"

He shrugged, stuck an unlit cigar in his mouth, and headed toward the exit. "Yeah, honey. It worked fine."

Outside, a small group of people were gathered around a mint condition, early seventies (if I remember my cousin's Matchbox cars correctly) red Camaro. Of course it could only belong to "The Leslie," who paused briefly to answer a few questions about cubic inches and drivetrains or transmissions or something like that before brushing them off.

"You know, not many people go to a foreign country for the summer with empty suitcases," he said, tossing my luggage into the backseat. "I mean, I'm no genius or nothin', but you gotta figure you're gonna get stopped at customs." He laughed. "Am I right?"

There was a long pause as we drove away. I had decided not to engage "The Leslie" in conversation until further notice. Unfortunately, he was not through

"Uh, listen. I hope you don't mind, but I gotta make a quick stop at my friend Jimmy's place."

I hesitated. "Is it on the way?"

"Everything's on the way in Paris, honey," Leslie said, chuckling.

chapter two

Chez Mwah!

date: A SHORT TIME LATER

mood: EMBRACE YOUR DREAM!

＊　＊　＊

At the sight of Galleries Lafayette, my soul exploded into untold googles of happiness. Immense awe overwhelmed me and inner squeals gave way to waves of unfathomable bliss mixed with a tad of motion sickness. (Don't bother visualizing whirred peas or anything.)

By the time Leslie had screeched to a halt in front of a little red Smart Car, we were late. *(Quelle surprise!)* And I was ready for CPR.

I set Toy, tail wagging like mad, onto the sidewalk and took a look around. Deep, cool shade tinged with glistening sunlight dotted the rows of old, ivy-covered town houses. A warm breeze rustled through blossoming chestnut trees that lined the street, and everything that had happened in my life up until now disappeared. I was in heaven. Though I hadn't been here for nearly a year, it was exactly the same. Paris sat timeless and mythical in a changeless present. It was a beautiful city, full of mansard roofs, double-height curved windows, sculpted limestone facades with decorative wrought-iron balconies. It was a place where the people went about their business in the way that only French people can—with quiet dignity and pride.

Aunt Tamara's little jewel box of a house was nestled right in the middle of one of the most charming old blocks in Paris. As I stared up at the darlingest house on not only the block, but an entire city full of darling and charming, it came to me. Aunt Tamara's house would henceforth be known as *Chez Mwah*!!

"Girlena!" Evie (fashion phylum: *The P.I.T.s*) shouted, bounding down the front steps. "Where *have* you been?!"

Instead of the more classical greeting—you know, hugs and air kisses—Evie huffed, "I've been waiting here for hours!" In truth it had been less than twenty minutes, but that was Evie for you—prone to exaggeration. Just like her clothes. She wore a sporty white sleeveless jacket over a lime green striped sequined tank top, calf-hugging leggings, a yellow-and-white logo visor and a pair of green-and-white-striped peep-toe pumps. (Evie reminds us that fashion rules are meant to be broken.)

Although she was a very pretty girl, her exotic beauty wasn't the common sort you'd find in a town like Greenwich, where regular good looks and oceans of blond ponytails prevailed. I, for one, particularly admired Evie's beauty. It was an unusual combination, due to a Japanese father and a Jewish, by way of Eastern Europe, mother.

Evie was petite. Her weight fluctuated like the seasons, as she was a chronic yo-yo dieter. She was freckly, like me, with sea green eyes, long dark hair, a smallish nose, and a wide, toothy smile. With her attitude and individualism, and the fact that we were kindred fashion spirits — not to mention we were both only children, our friendship had grown so over the years that we were pretty much inseparable.

I flipped up my white heart-shaped shades and whispered, "I was hijacked—"

"I told you we'd make it in one piece," Leslie interrupted, dropping my bags on the sidewalk between us.

Evie stepped back, regarding him suspiciously, and said, "And you are?"

"*This* is Leslie. Aunt Tamara's housekeeper."

"You're Leslie?" she said, gawking. "I thought she was a woman—I mean . . . no offense."

"Hey, no harm, no foul. I'm not a sensitive guy."

He eyed Evie's outfit with obvious wonder and chuckled. "Hey, I'll bet nobody ever lost you in a crowd."

"Or you," she murmured, getting acquainted with his vibe.

Sensing a hint of tension between them, I attempted

to change the subject to our favorite topic: fashion!!

"Nice tracksuit, by the way."

"Yeah." He smiled, biting down on his cigar. "I always wear Prada."

"But it says Adidas. Right there," I said, pointing to the logo above his heart.

"Trust me, honey, it's Prada. Now, if you ladies don't mind, I gotta be someplace in a hurry. I'll be back in an hour. And don't make plans for tonight—I've got a great dinner in store for youse."

With that, he headed for his car.

"Hey"—Leslie turned back, threw me a set of keys, and chuckled—"I almost forgot. Your chariot awaits, milady."

I caught the keys, totally bewildered.

"But Mom and Dad said it would be too expensive to ship my Vespa, and that I'd just have to use public transportation to get around."

"Your aunt arranged for something else," he said, pointing to the little red Smart Car he'd blocked in at the curb. "*That* is what you'll be driving this summer."

"*That's* a real car?!" Evie gasped. "It looks like a toy!"

"Your aunt thought you'd need some wheels this summer, so she lent you hers. Take good care of it," he said, bounding off.

"Hey, what about my luggage?!" I hollered after him.

"Don't worry, *Georges* will take care of it."

Faster than a New York minute, he was gone.

I turned to Evie and shrugged, and we both started laughing. "And I was worried about being supervised."

After we'd thoroughly checked out the new wheels, we grabbed the bags on the sidewalk and followed Toy up the steps, inside Chez Mwah.

"Where's all your stuff?" I asked.

"I think Georges"—pronounced *zhorzh*—"is taking it upstairs."

"Oh," I gasped, "you've already met Georges."

"Of course. We're old friends now."

I dropped my suitcases next to some of Evie's stuff in the foyer. Evie's "stuff" amounted to a slightly smaller version of the Matterhorn. Dress forms, an antique Louis Vuitton steamer trunk, a full set of Fendi luggage, plastic-covered fabric bolts from Lesage (France's oldest and most treasured hand embroiderer), Desrues (a costume jewelry and button maker), Lemarié (for feathers galore), and Michel (the chicest hat maker in Paris), were piled skyward. And of course, a box filled with her rare stuffed animal collection, which she never leaves home without. I felt a sudden tinge of empathy for Georges.

"C'mon," Evie chirped. "He's probably in the apartment."

She laced her arm though mine and we headed upstairs. A potent cocktail of smelly cheese, operatic vocal scales, bouillabaisse, and Edith Piaf records filled the air as we climbed the winding, wrought-iron-and-marble staircase to the top floor. At the landing stood a small, wafer-thin man.

"Bonjour," he said in a semiformal, clipped tone. His hair was a tad unkempt and grayish—more salt than pepper. But

his gait, I noticed as we walked toward the apartment at the end of the hallway, was that of a young man.

I opted for my native tongue. "Hi. I'm Imogene."

This stopped him in his tracks.

"Ah, oui, Mademoiselle Eeemozheeen," he said, bowing slightly, as he held my hand. *"Enchanté."* And kissed it.

Did I mention he oozed charm?

"Hello again, Georges," Evie said. She glanced at me and smiled. "Georges simply *loves* my *on-som-blay.* Don't you, Georges?"

He paused briefly to reflect. Then, with a raised eyebrow, he said, "It eez difficult to express my feelings regarding your 'on-sem-blay.'"

We spent the rest of the afternoon unpacking. The first thing I did was affix my master clothing inventory map to the inside wall of the walk-in closet. Said list detailed, down to the last Alexandre de Paris hair clip, everything I owned, should my Imogenius SoftWear program fail and I have to switch to manual dress mode— perish the thought. Let me explain. Necessity being the mother of invention (and I'm nothing if not inventive), I vowed to forever eradicate those spiritually demoralizing I-can't-believe-I-wore-that moments from the lives of girls everywhere. To that end I enlisted the help of Cissy de Winter, one of my nearest and dearest school friends, not to mention the most scientifically gifted star of the GCA Computer Programming Society. Together we developed *Imogenius* SoftWear, a program that preassembles the "perfect outfit" every time, with nothing more than a few simple keystrokes on your PDA or mobile phone. All that's required are a few digital photographs of one's wardrobe and accessories, along with some personal but essential details such as moods, astrological sign, and hormonal fluctuations. And of course, it also came with a personal closet consultation with *moi*. Before you can say "virtual stylist," out pops your ideal outfit—head to toe! It even suggests beauty products!

"Voilà! No major brain cell expenditure required!!" Cissy exclaimed when we were done.

True! I mean, think about it, no more firsthand embarrassment when deliberating over the perfect look. No matter whether you've had a major fight with the parents over your monthly cell phone bill or you're in a tizzy over having broken up with your boyfriend twice in one day. Or other times, when you're absolutely unable to decide between Chanel's Lilac Sky (happy days) or Vamp (PMS days); or what to wear for a casual luncheon on the Avenue with the BFFs. It's completely infallible every time.

"It's also very convenient for we Greenwich girls," I added, feeling quite philanthropic (a natural inbred Greenwich trait). "And for a nominal licensing fee, we'll never have to worry about poverty again!"

"What's poverty?" Cissy asked.

Anyway, *Imogenius*, as we called it, caught on like bedbugs at the Helmsley. Before you could say "ka-ching," everyone at GCA was swearing by it (and wearing by it)! I mean, it was the absolute greatest feeling. Suddenly I had beaucoup bucks—enough that it's made a complete mini-mogul out of me. I've even started my own charitable foundation—the SPFA (Society for the Prevention of Fashion Angst).

Back to the closet. I filled one side with my newest A-list outfits: the Alber Elbazes, Balenciagas, and Chanels. My B-list outfits—categorized mostly as last year's stuff—were placed on the other side. Urban bikinis (aka jeans) were placed on shelves one, two, and three. Tank tops sat on shelf three, row F. Shoes were lined up like soldiers along the bottom of the four walls. And dresses were hung, color coded, throughout.

By the time evening rolled around I was so exhausted I barely had enough energy to chew my food. Despite the fact that Leslie's "flower dinner"—lavender-crusted duck, poppy zucchini carpaccio, and a delish dessert of raspberry and violet tartlettes—was completely wonderful.

It turned out, Leslie's big rush earlier was to get to cooking class! A future gastropreneur, he was enrolled at Le Cordon Bleu and had hopes of opening his own restaurant some day.

After dinner, with—thankfully—nothing left to do, Evie and I headed back upstairs, and I threw all the pillows on the floor and relaxed. Evie dumped a mini shopping bag of Bourjois makeup in between us. She broke out a stash of Debauve & Gallais chocolates, and we blushed, glossed, gobbled, and gossiped. She regaled me with the latest about her internship in the buttons, embroideries, and embellishments room at the House of Lamour.

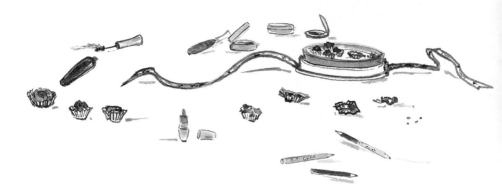

"I'm still pinching myself," she gushed. "Yesterday Crispin *himself* asked to see samples of my work. I guess my biweekly classes in French hand embroidery at l'École Lesage are starting to pay off because—get this—he told me that my stitching was *incroyable*!"

"He said that?! *Incroyable*?!" We shrieked in unison. (It doesn't take much to whip us into a frenzy!)

Unfortunately, our shrieks of joy triggered a series of rapid footsteps that pounded down the hall and burst the door open. Leslie stood there, eyes bulging, wooden spoon at the ready.

"What's going on in here?!" he huffed breathlessly, while searching the room suspiciously with his eyes. "Are you guys okay?"

"Of course we're okay. Why wouldn't we be?" I asked.

"I thought I heard screaming."

"That was happy screaming."

"Which is completely different from scared screaming. Duh!" Evie added.

"Happy screaming, huh? My mistake," he grumbled and

jerked the door shut. Evie and I stared at each other for a second, then screamed with laughter.

But laughing with Evie reminded me how sad I was. (We Greenwich girls are slightly backward, after all.) And somewhere between chatting about my parents and discussing Evie's new diet, a "Paolo Pang," otherwise known as "The Pangs," broke through. This was a relatively new phenomenon that had begun when Paolo and I decided to spend our summer apart. Symptoms included, but were not limited to, obsessively checking e-mail a gazillion times a day for messages from said Pang inducer, paranoid speculation concerning his whereabouts, emphatic petit fours consumption, sporadic reading of Sylvia Plath poetry, excessive lip glossage, and frequent urges to burst into tears at the drop of a hat. So far I had managed to handle things fairly well, convincing myself that it was only a matter of time before I'd calm down and start feeling better. Unfortunately, the exact opposite had happened and now my symptoms were getting worse. I sat there desperately trying not to think about you-know-who; trying not to spoil the moment for Evie. But she knew. After all, she wasn't my best friend for nothing.

"It's time to let it out, girlene," she said ruefully, pushing a box of tissues toward me.

I yanked a few out, recited a silent mantra to the goddess of strength, and took the plunge.

"The thing of it is," I heaved, "when I told Paolo about this chance to spend the summer in Paris, I was so excited. I mean, I couldn't *wait* to go. But then the strangest thing happened — he didn't object. He didn't even bat an eye. I mean, I thought he'd declare his undying love for me, then tell me how miserable he'd be without me . . . at the very least try to talk me out of it. But he just looked at me coldly and said, 'I think spending the summer in Paris will be a great experience for you, Imogene.'"

I started to feel that feeling that I was going to lose it any second, so I walked to the window and stuck my head out, hoping to chill out.

From the window, I could see boats twinkling on the Seine. The Eiffel Tower was ablaze in red, white, and blue lights, and the Arc de Triomphe sparkled brighter than a gazillion Cartier diamonds.

The view, rather than distracting me, overwhelmed my senses, and a first tear pushed through. I jammed a tissue into my eye, trying to hold back the impending deluge, because once I let loose we'd need an ark to stay dry.

"I just don't understand it. Paolo's in Italy with his family," I warbled, "and I'm in Paris — and I don't know if we'll ever see each other again!"

That thought released the floodgates. Big-time.

"I try not to think about him," I hiccupped, "but I just can't help it. I miss his smile, his broken English, and how he'd tease me about little things. And I mean all last week, I'd just be sitting in Starbucks, sipping a cappuccino, and wham — I'd completely lose it. Whenever a Ferrari zoomed by" — (a common occurrence in Greenwich) — "whack!

I'd turn to Jell-O. And when Mom asked me to pick up a bottle of Italian olive oil at the market—kablam! Destroyed. Anything and everything Italian reminded me of Paolo!"

Evie wandered over to the window and took a deep breath of summer evening. I sniffled into my tissue. "Question," she said, with a smidge of attitude, "where are you right now?"

"Lost? Wandering aimlessly through an emotional abyss . . . a shadow of my former self?"

"I don't mean emotionally."

"You don't?" I sniffed.

"Listen, girlena, there are lots of other guys out there. Not that I know any of them," she added as an afterthought, under her breath. "I mean, I've lost ten pounds and I'm still single. All that agony and suffering and it's all going to waste."

"You just haven't met the right person yet," I said, trying through my own despair to be encouraging.

"Do you have any idea how many times I've heard that? From you, from my mother, my cousins, my aunts, my grandparents?"

"You left out your father." I chuckled sadly.

Evie and I had the opposite problem. She needed to find someone, and I needed to find myself.

"I don't even know who I am anymore. We spent so much time with each other over the last year it's as though I'm not a whole person without him. Like I'm missing a body part or something. Or like I'm missing me."

"You've lost your identity, girlena," Evie said with some

authority. "Like many before you, you've been pulled into the 'we' vortex."

"The what?"

"You know, the place where two people meld into one and cease to be individuals. Maybe this is exactly the thing you both needed. A reason to be apart."

"A reason to break up," I sobbed.

Evie slid next to me with a supportive hug. Eventually, having waded through a box of tissues and a dozen champagne truffles, I was semi-myself again. But then, Evie dropped the A-bomb.

"I think now would be a good time for me to tell you something," she said with some hesitation. "I didn't want to mention this before, because I didn't want to see you hurt, but I need to tell you."

"What do you mean?" I asked as my heart slowed down.

"My dear girlena," Evie said, "I suggest you sit down for what I'm about to tell you." She took my hand and led me back to the cushions on the floor, where we'd been sitting earlier. "To put it bluntly, your Paolo isn't quite the angel you think he is."

A stab of numbness shot up my legs.

"Paolo hasn't been completely honest with you regarding a certain mutual friend of ours."

"And who would that be?" I asked.

Evie then opened a dresser drawer that she'd earlier consigned her underwear to, and unfolded a ragged piece of white copy paper. It looked as if it had been folded and refolded a thousand times. With the most pitiful look on her face, she took a deep breath and handed it to me. "Saffron sent me this e-mail last week."

Despite the fact that I was beyond perplexed, I began reading the e-mail from our GCA classmate.

To: Evie

Fr: Saffron

Subject: URGENT!

Re: Imogene & Paolo

 I have some bad news regarding Imogene, and I don't know what to do. I could never hurt her feelings, so please don't say a word of this, but today, as I was walking up Greenwich Avenue, I saw with my own eyes—right outside Tiffany's—Paolo giving Priscilla a little Tiffany's gift box! Of course I immediately hid behind the brick wall so they wouldn't see me.

But when I peeked back around, Paolo had his arm around her shoulder. They were laughing, and it looked like they were making some kind of plans. He wrote something down on a piece of paper and gave it her, but before I could hear anything else, they ducked into Terra. . . .

There was more, but I had read enough. My knees were weak. I felt as if the rug had been dragged out from under me. All I wanted to do was crawl under the covers and go to sleep. And never wake up again!

Suddenly it all made sense. How aloof he'd become lately. How unemotional he was when I told him about Paris. Now

I realized it was because he'd found someone else. And he didn't have either the heart, or the temerity, to tell me. He was probably waiting for me to leave, counting the days, so he could continue his fling with Priscilla. For all I knew, maybe he wasn't even going to Italy. The RAT!!

I returned the paper to Evie, divided between tears and smiles.

"Why didn't you tell me?"

"I didn't want to hurt you, but now seeing you suffer over someone who doesn't seem to care about your feelings, I had to tell you. So that you can move on," she said, trying to read my face for emotion. I could see she was asking herself if she'd done the right thing by telling me.

"I know it hurts now. But look on the bright side. Maybe Paolo and you were ultimately not meant to be. Maybe your future dream guy is right here, in Paris!"

I tried to still my brain, though my body was shaking. Have I forgotten my most important mantra? I asked myself. Put your trust in fate. I've always trusted fate to do the right thing by me, and it's never let me down.

"Listen," Evie said, "my parents are going back to New York in the morning. They're leaving me the key to their hotel suite. I can use their expense account anytime I want. So starting tomorrow you and I are going to go absolutely crazy!"

I smiled limply and wiped away the last trace of tears.

"Shopping, sight-seeing, and the best food in the world. But best of all," she grinned slyly, "boy watching."

It wasn't long before jet lag and the day and night's dramas gave way to overwhelming exhaustion. I passed out as soon as my head hit the pillow and dreamed of Paolo all night long.

June 19

6:00 a.m.

To: Priscilla

Fr: Imogene

Re: Subscription Cancellation

Dear Priscilla,

Due to circumstances beyond my control, aka cheating, we un-regretfully inform you that your *Imogenius* subscription is hereby canceled. Effective immediately. Please direct any further inquiries to super-rat Paolo Glamonti.

Sincerely,

Your ex-friend,

Imogene

I t being our maiden day in Paris, Evie and I got an early start. Since you never get a second chance to make a first impression, I fired up my little Imogenius. Unlike last summer, when I was the "rich little poor girl," I opted for a new alter ego, trying "rich little rich girl" on for size.

We spent the day shopping and getting reacquainted with the city. Somehow Paris in the morning inspired utterly base-less optimism. Everywhere, everything throbbed with life. At outdoor cafés friends air kissed hello, bubble-blowing children strolled with their nannies through the *jardins*, and chic women and their dogs got tangled in their dog leashes. This, and more, stimulated waves of pleasurable endorphins in my brain. A strong sense of anticipation filled me with the innate knowledge that anything was possible, and I knew with certainty that something exciting would soon happen. Despite Paolo. I was tuned in with the universe with all the power of my destiny. It seeped through my every pore, and I was on high alert for signs of its impending manifestation.

While shopping, I made out like a bandit, scoring a bunch of old French makeup cases, a pair of whimsical Lacroix heart-shaped earrings (let the cuteness begin!), and a circa 1959 Kelly bag.

(*Random quote: I can resist everything except temptation.*)

We said good-bye to Evie's parents at the hotel and stayed on for a late lunch. Then, again, we shopped, shopped, shopped until Toy flopped and we dropped. Well, almost. Paris seemed to be having a remarkably strange effect on Evie. I mean, she was becoming *completely* boy-crazy. That, combined with her desire to get my mind off of you-know-who, amounted to a not-so-subtle effort to point out every cute guy within a five-foot radius. I must admit, though, it was pretty hysterical at times and it cheered me up a lot.

Outside of Le Bon Marché, a hormonally crazed Evie introduced herself (and me) to a totally French *jeune homme*. Gerard, as he turned out to be, was their window dresser, who just *happened* to be standing there admiring his handiwork. Evie and I stood beside him and admired his work too, which was nothing short of a masterpiece. He told us he had dedicated the window to the upcoming Couture

Week. The display featured the entire history of fashion, from cave rags to *recherché*. Gerard seemed very interested in Evie. He took her number and assured her he'd call her later.

After dinner we took Toy for a long walk along the Seine, where a brief smidge of melancholy—a combination of jet lag, a surprising tinge of homesickness for the parents, and boyfriend dejection—unexpectedly bubbled up inside me.

After a silent attempt to further unravel my feelings, we went back home to Chez Mwah and wound up watching *The Godfather* with Leslie and eating his own version of French Cracker Jacks—Délicieux!

As for Gerard? Well, he did call.

All in all it was a joyous day.

chapter three

The P.i.t.s vs. The Wolfe Pack

date: JUNE 20
daily obsession: PINK

I have a pathological weakness for pink. I've always felt that wearing pink helps one exude the bubbliest of attitudes. I mean, how can one be as full of optimism as moi, and not love pink?

✳   ✳   ✳

I was having kittens, driving Aunt Tamara's adorable Smart Car through the cobblestone streets on my way to Hautelaw Paris (HLP). Smart Car is definitely a Paris advantage. I had a random thought: If I were watching me zooming along some *rue* in Paris, I would have to say that I was the epitome of cuteness.

My first day of work was divided into three parts.

One: Pick up swatches and samples from the list of booths at Première Vision that Mick gave me. Two: Start camcording Parisian chic-ies and store windows. Three: Start organizing the office. Having finished the first two, it was time to hit HLP.

I hit a pothole as I turned onto the Quai—the promenade that runs along the Seine. According to Spring, HLP occupied a little office there. I just knew it would be the most charming thing I ever saw. On the left, rows of poplar-shaded cafés and shops nestled beneath a potpourri of apartment buildings from the twenties and thirties. To the right, adorable little houseboats of every size and shape were fitted end to end along a narrow wooden pier that traced the river's edge. What, I asked myself, could be more perfect? Or more French? I imagined myself sitting in my impossibly chic office looking down at the street below at the quaint shops and houseboats on the river, then out over the lush vista of Paris in the summer.

I pushed my *Paris for Dummies* book back into the glove compartment and whipped out the roughly scribbled map Georges had made for me. According to the map, No. 226e commanded full views of the Musée de l'Orangerie, the Jardin des Tuileries, and the Eiffel Tower. As I cruised down the block amid these and other idyllic visions looking for No. 226e, I noted one small but inescapable problem. All the even numbers were on the right-hand side of the street—the river side. The houseboat side. I briefly contemplated driving to the end of the block and turning around in hopes of reversing the numbers, but settled for a more sane option — slow down. I studied Georges's map, mentally retracing my route to ensure that I followed the directions exactly. This just couldn't be right. Could it?

I mean, one wouldn't equate the word "backward" with anything having to do with the French, though I have noticed a few strange anomalies since arriving. For instance, in Paris, *dames* are not chicks or broads or even young girls. They're old. *Concierges* are not hotel workers but apartment building superintendents. Even though it's the oldest bridge in Paris the Pont Neuf means "new bridge." The Place de la Concorde, "Place of harmony," is anything but — that's where they chopped off Marie Antoinette's head! Although the majority of waiters in Paris are over forty years old, they are called *garçons* — which means "boy." Graffiti is an art form. The Left Bank of the Seine, or Rive Gauche, is actually the south bank, and the right bank, the Rive Droite, is actually the north bank! And then there's the word *haute*. If you're a devout reader, you'll know that the word *haute* is pronounced "out" (especially if you're from Canada). But in reality, it's totally "in."

Thankfully, being a Greenwich native, I'm an old hand at backward thinking, so it took me no time to get used to the Paris brain.

I gawked at what could *only* be described as the worst house in the 'hood. It was like the old eyesore at the end of the block with the dead weeds in the yard and darkened windows. You know the one — nobody lives there anymore, or if they do you never really find out, and don't want to because they're probably really weird and scary. I mean, the place was more than a few shingles short of *House & Garden*. For starters, it hadn't had a coat of paint since Marie Antoinette lost her head over a slice of *gâteau*. I mean, there was more peeling going on than at a Beverly Hills skin clinic. Not to mention several layers of dirt, broken shutters, and a missing railing or three.

"Okay, don't panic," I said aloud, attempting to look on the bright side. It *was* a houseboat. And it *was* on the Seine. And it *did* have an Eiffel Tower view.

I poked the little metal numbers tacked to the mailbox in hopes that the 6 was really an upside-down 9 that had come loose—no such luck.

After several more minutes of indecision I managed to will myself down the dock, up the rickety steps, and onto the boat or, more to the point, shipwreck. The houseboat was a long, rectangular, and had an uneven roof that, judging from the precarious ladder attached to the side, had some sort of deck on top. Although I absolutely refused to go up there for fear of falling through the ceiling. A narrow walkway circled the perimeter and widened into generous decks at either end.

I lifted my digital camcorder out of my bag and stepped through a pair of decrepit plantation shutters that passed for doors, sidled down a hallway, and found myself in what must have been the living room in a former lifetime. Even though it was a bit dark, I began shooting. Through my lens, I saw a pair of grimy picture windows that faced the

Seine. In an attempt to rally the eternal optimist in me I began talking—rationalizing things, like: "It isn't so bad," and "This could be a lot worse," and anything else I could think of to lift my rapidly sinking spirits. I mean, it did have good bones, after all. And in the world of fashion, good bones are everything. It just needed a smidge of TLC. Okay, gobs of it!

For some reason the room began to remind me a little of Paolo's East Village dorm room slash apartment (before he moved in) so my slightly elevated demeanor began to take a nosedive. In order to avoid an oncoming attack of the Pangs, I resolved to check out the rest of the boat. But as I spun around the room, shooting one last swirling panoramic view with the camcorder, I ran smack into *something*, which turned out to be a *someone*, which made me scream at the top of my lungs. I jumped backward, nearly cracking my skull open on a wide beam that ran the length of the room. Did I mention it had low ceilings?

"Hey!!" I said.

"I'm sorry," he said, "I didn't mean to startle you."

He was tall and sweaty, and he was covered from head to toe in dirt. He looked about nineteen, with blondish hair, and he was holding a pry bar.

"What the hell are you doing sneaking around here?!"

"Is your head all right?"

"No! My head is *not* all right!" I snapped, rubbing the fast-rising instant baseball-size lump on my cranium.

He looked up at the ceiling thoughtfully. "I'll make a note to get rid of those beams."

"And you haven't answered my question!"

"You must be Imogene. I'm Dax," he said with the slightest French accent, extending his hand. "Spring did not tell you I was coming?"

"No, Spring did *not* tell me you were coming," I said, shoving the camcorder back into my bag.

"I'm here to do the renovations," he added, dropping his hand awkwardly.

"How do I know you're not some squatter?"

"Squatter? What is squatter?"

"Squatter, as in someone who camps out in places that don't belong to them. You know, *trespass*."

"Trespass?"

"Would you mind not repeating everything I say?"

He went silent after that, so we just stared at each other while I debated whether to scream for the police or drive myself to the emergency hospital when my phone rang. I shot him the old "do you *mind*" glare, and he wandered off to parts unknown.

"Imogene, dahhhhhling!" Spring's voice bellowed from across an ocean. "I wanted to give you enough time to get to the new office before calling. Are you there yet?"

"Yes, I'm here."

"Fabulous! Did you find it all right?"

"Um. It's hard to miss," I said trying to sound as positive and nonchalant as possible.

"Good! Wonderful!"

"Did you, by any chance, hire someone named Dax?"

"Who, dear?"

"Dax. That's who he claims to be, anyway."

"Oh, *Dax*, of course! Wonderful boy! Always has been! Dax is going to do the restorations. You know, spruce things up a bit."

"So, you do *know* him?"

"Who, dear?"

"Dax!"

"*Know him?* Sweetie, he's Herve's son! I've known him since he was a toddler."

"Who's Herve?"

"Herve was my third husband . . . or was it fifth? I can never remember. I haven't seen him since he was twelve! Is he still adorable?"

I made a clean spot on the window and peered through on the off chance Dax might be out there doing whatever it was he was supposed to be doing. Sure enough, he was busy ripping hunks of Precambrian Astroturf off the deck. Okay, so he didn't look like a vagrant — he appeared to be more studious. And was a tad hunkier. Not that I had any interest whatsoever.

"Imogene, are you still there?" Spring's voice called from somewhere nearby. I stared at my cell phone.

"Yes . . . yes, I'm here. We must have a bad connection."

"So tell me." Spring took a long drag from her cigarette, then whispered with great anticipation, "How is it?"

"How is what?"

"The space, dahling! The future home of Hautelaw Pareee?"

42

"It's a little . . . boatlike."

"Of course it's boatlike. It's a boat, sweetie. I did say it was on the Seine, didn't I?"

"But it's *in* the Seine."

"On, in—what's the difference? Hold on, sweetie . . . the boys just came in."

Spring was referring to Hautelaw's peerless creative director, Mick, their fabulous and somewhat flamboyant art director, Malcolm, and his assistant, Ian. They made up my support group at work and had been incredible last summer, helping me learn the industry ropes and keeping me spiritually afloat through my own personal travesties and demi-dramas.

There was a sudden loud pop, followed by an eardrum-piercing electronic shriek, as Spring switched to speaker-phone.

"Are you still there, dear?" Spring's over-amped voice thundered into my ear.

I jerked the phone to arm's length and hollered, "Still here!"

"Wonderful! Mick has some things he wants to tell you."

"Bonjour, chérie!"

"Hi, Mick."

"Listen, I want to remind you that we're starting to assemble next season's book and we'll be needing your 'on-the-street' coverage soon."

"Oh, right. I already have some ideas! In fact, I was just thinking last night that—"

"And FYI, dahling," Spring interrupted, "*everyone* is doing the 'tourist chic' thing this year. Again!!"

"Tourist chic?" I echoed, trying to sound as jaded as possible. "How embarrassing! I mean, that is *sooo* tired!"

"Nobody imagines for a minute you would produce anything of *that* caliber," Malcolm added.

"Me?!" I chuckled nervously. "Never!!"

Mental note: Nix "tourist chic" document on desktop.

"Needless to say," Spring drawled, "after last summer's *spectacular* coverage, everyone here is waiting with bated breath for your next brilliant idea! I just know you'll send us something positively . . . *genius*!"

Spring began laughing uproariously and the boys followed suit—as did her two pugs (barking, I mean). For my part, all I could think about was how I was going to top last year's coverage.

"Now I've got to go. I'm late for my Thermage appointment with Dr. Pat," she puffed. "*À tout à l'heure!*"

Click. She was gone. I was on my own again. With the houseboat a shambles, and nowhere to work, I figured I'd hit the streets and start working up some trend stories. On the way out, I spotted Dax and figured I might as well say good-bye—he was, after all, Herve's son. Had I been a hair too harsh with him? Maybe I was taking my anger at Paolo out on him. Whatever the reason, he was going to be around for the summer, so we might as well be friends.

"Well, I guess I'll be seeing you around," I said, slipping on my sunglasses.

Dax frowned.

"What is it?"

"Nothing," he said quietly, looking down at his feet.

"Look." I sighed. "I'm sorry I got upset with you. . . ."

"Oh, it's not that."

"What then?"

"Well, if I were you I wouldn't wear those," he said, gently tapping the top of my glasses.

"Why?"

"Because hiding those eyes behind sunglasses is like hanging a Monet painting in a closet."

"I . . . ummm . . . well, I . . ."

Talk about being caught off guard! And what does a girl like *moi* do with unexpected compliments? She gets flustered, takes a step backward, and trips over a pile of Precambrian Astroturf. How firsthand embarrassing!

Dax suppressed a smile and extended his hand to me for the second time that day. "Have you ever seen the Eiffel Tower at sunset?"

I love how every big city seems to have a special place where its over-urbanized citizens go to chill. Like Central Park. I like to think of it as an island of paradise amid a raging storm of commerce. I mean, it's the one niche in New York where an office-weary populace can shake off the dust of conference calls and customer satisfaction with a nice leisurely jog, or a bike ride, or even, dare I say, a quiet canoodle on the grass.

As it turned out, the same was true in Paris, where local denizens gathered beneath the Eiffel Tower for what they quaintly referred to as *les rollers* —a weekly shindig of relaxation, romance, and Roller-blading. And with half the youth of Paris in one place, it was the perfect opportunity to scope out the latest and greatest in street trends up close and personal.

Dax reached for my hand as I alighted from the curb in a cloud of Miss Dior Chérie and a pair of rented in-line skates. I hit the power button on my camera and breezed into the crowd, shooting randomly as I sailed along, recording for all posterity the proclivities of contemporary French fashion finicky-ness in hopes of stumbling onto the next big trend before the book deadline.

While we were waiting for Evie and Gerard, I took the opportunity to get to know Dax a little better. First and foremost, he was an Aquarius. For those of you who don't have their astrological charts handy, Aquarians are known for their honesty, intelligence, and out-of-the-box thinking. So it was not surprising that, rather than a derelict, he turned out to be an architecture student whose mother was (*zut alors!*) American. Apparently, while traveling through Provence one summer, she had met and married his father—a former diplomat to Spain. Anyway, he wound up going to school in Paris, where he and his friends did carpentry during the summers—picking up piecework wherever they could. When Dax got wind of the houseboat renovation, he went into high gear, convincing Herve, who convinced Spring that with his talent and combined resources the houseboat would be nothing short of a masterpiece. This, of course, remained to be seen, but I determined, as Spring's official representative overseas, to keep a close eye on him.

Evie and Gerard joined us at sunset for a few laps around the tower. When they first pulled up she was sliding all over the place, hanging on to Gerard for support and claiming to be terrible on wheels. I say "claiming" because two very short years ago Evie did the Venice Beach Diet, a strict program consisting of diced avocados, isolation tank therapy, and Rollerblading—lots and lots of Rollerblading. And it worked. For a while, anyway. I mean, aside from the fact that Evie won't be able to look an avocado in the eye for at least a century, she did manage to lose eight pounds, reach nirvana, and became such a good skater she was asked to play left wing on the GCA street hockey team, which she politely refused but did do a nice redesign of their uniform.

Evie's eyes flashed at Dax, followed by a quick, lascivious smile in my direction, which I totally ignored. Not because it wasn't perfectly understandable—even, dare I say, flattering. But right then, with all the sparkle and vivacity of Paris spinning around me in joyous celebration, it was upsetting. I mean, aside from almost triggering another attack of the Pangs, it made me realize that not only was I incapable of shaking off the past, I was equally incapable of living in the present. Which left only the future. And since I always leave that to fate, there didn't seem to be anywhere left to go. Except sideways, of course. Which is exactly where I went.

I zipped into the crowd, madly camcording in an attempt to derail my feelings. I had just locked on to a Balenciaga couple channeling Madonna (circa '04) with McQueen overtones and was feeling a little less overwhelmed when *BLAM!* I was blindsided by someone, or, as I soon discovered, some-THING that sent me sprawling onto the pavement.

"I'm sooooooooooooooooooo sorry!" oozed a familiar English accent.

"Oh, look, Fern," a second English accent piped in.

"That looks like what's-her-face from that low-rent forecasting company around the corner."

"I believe you're correct, Romaine. I'd recognize that skating style anywhere."

While they cackled at this, a pair of hands gently lifted me to my feet.

"Are you hurt?" Dax said, glaring at Fern and Romaine Snipes (aka the Salad Sisters; fashion phylum: The *Wolfe Pack*), as they slowly circled us like a pair of hungry sharks.

"I don't think so," I grumbled, rubbing my arm.

"Hey!" Evie zoomed up with Gerard. "I saw that!"

"Oh, look, Fern." Romaine chuckled. "It's the goth girl scout to the rescue."

"You mean the one who *thinks* she's a designer?" Fern asked caustically.

"If you call that designing," Romaine snipped, stopping in front of Evie, studying her face carefully. "Hey," she said. "Isn't she the girl who plastered you with Crème de la Mer in Barneys last year?"

Romaine skated over and gawked at Evie for a while.

"I smell wood burning," Evie murmured.

Romaine's eyes suddenly lit up as she gasped in horror. "OH-MY-GAWD! You're right!"

She lurched forward, but Gerard slipped between them.

"Let's all play nice, shall we?" He smiled.

"Leave her alone, girls," a voice purred behind us. "She can't help being a dork."

I spun around and there, emanating major "tough-girl chic," was Brooke, sending me hate vibes at a trillion miles an hour. Her true essence was on display in (Cavalli) snakeskin. She wore a tight bomber jacket and matching capris. Aside from going completely tanorexic and strategically smudging her eyeliner for that smoldering après-you-know-what look, Brooke hadn't changed much at all since I had last seen her. Her otherwise disposable smile was still intact and fully operational. As for her demeanor, well, that definitely hadn't changed.

The memory of last summer stung my brain. Brooke was the girl I had replaced after she tried to steal (among other things) my cell phone and then my would-be boyfriend, Paolo, and sell my coverage elsewhere, and then lie her way out of it by blaming me. After being broomed from Hautelaw, she wound up at the competition—aka Haute & About, which, as it so happens, is headed by Spring's lifelong nemesis, the nefarious Winter Tan—a woman whose reputation for stealing ideas (Spring's and/or anyone else's, for that matter) was legend on Fashion Avenue.

"Well, if it isn't little Dorothy," Brooke said, smiling acidly. "And look, girls, she has a new boyfriend." She paused for dramatic effect, furrowing her brow in mock concern. "Don't tell me you got tired of the Italian stallion already?"

My incredibly well-trained mind leaped into action with a centering affirmation: *I radiate peace and serenity no matter what is going on around me.*

It didn't work.

"What are you doing here?" I heaved.

"We were about to ask you the very same question," sneered Candy Wolfe as she slid next to Brooke. Now the Wolfe Pack was complete.

Candy Wolfe was the "leader" of the Wolfe Pack. She'd been Winter Tan's right-hand girl for a few years now, having alpha wolf status at Haute & About. A Ralph Lauren girl, she was dressed (as she'd seemed to be the one or two other times I'd seen her) quietly understated, in a navy-and-white-striped summer cashmere twin set and a pair of white capris.

"She's here because—" Evie began.

"I'm here for Couture Week," I interrupted, trying to prevent Evie from giving Brooke anything she could take back to her boss, "just doing coverage for Hautelaw. That's all."

"*Haute-house*? Who are they?" Candy asked innocently, bringing peals of laughter from Fern and Romaine.

"You know." Brooke smiled at me. "If you weren't so stupid, you might actually be clever. You see, we already know Spring is opening an office here, sweetie. Although why she sent *you* is a mystery."

"Yeah," Romaine snorted.

"Winter could care less about Spring's little business venture. Though, once she finds out you're in charge"—

Brooke tittered lightly—"I'm sure she'll sleep a little easier."

Dax looped his arm in mine. "Shall we go?"

"Oooooooh, boyfriend to the rescue! How charming," Brooke sneered.

"He's not my boyfriend," I snapped, jerking my arm away.

"Reaaalllly?" Brooke said. "Well, maybe he could be mine. Or I could call Paolo, now that he's free."

I must have lurched forward instinctively because Brooke suddenly jumped backward, almost falling over and taking Candy with her. Evie and I sniggered.

"Laugh it up, you little twerp!" Brooke seethed, frantically checking her hair. "You think you're so smart with that provincial schoolgirl routine of yours! You and your hapless little pal."

"Hapless?!" Evie shouted.

"As in loser," scoffed Candy.

Brooke did a quick check in her compact mirror, lowered her gaze at me, and spoke with icy calm. "Don't think I've forgotten last summer, Dorothy. You may have fooled Spring and the rest of those fashion failures at Hautelaw into thinking you're something special, but you didn't fool me. No doubt they're looking to you for some style revelation to stuff into their tawdry little forecasting book."

"What if they are?"

"Let me put it this way, sweetie. Paris can be a small town in many ways, and news travels fast. Especially fashion news. Which means it's practically impossible to discover the latest and greatest without someone else beating you to it."

"Meaning?"

"Meaning, Winter has asked me to 'staff up,' for the summer season. And to that end, I've hired a small army of trend spotters whose sole business it is to scour every club, every street fair, every concert, every museum, and every café in this burg for the latest and greatest. In other words, wherever you go looking for your *revelation*, we will already have been there. And *poor* Spring! I don't need to tell you how fickle *she* can be. I mean, once she recovers from the humiliation of being outdone by Winter, if she ever does, she's going to start having some serious doubts about her little prodigy. Like, maybe she's just another hick from the suburbs after all."

And with that parting shot, Brooke slid past Dax, running her hand lightly across his chest as she went and gazing into his eyes, putting that smudged eyeliner to use.

"You're yummy," she cooed. She flipped her head back to me. "I'll be sure to send Paolo your love." She blew a kiss and finished smugly with, "I believe I still have his number." Then she rolled off into the crowd.

Candy and Fern followed suit, but Romaine lingered for a second, circling Evie and Gerard like a hungry shark.

chapter four

I ♥ Paris

date: JULY 3

daily obsession: VINTAGE

An e-mail question from Pippa Potashnick re: advice on what to wear back home to her annual family reunion. I advised vintage. However, I believe that before one attempts a vintage vibe, one should aspire to master the rules of vintage etiquette—e.g., Grandma's triple-strand pearls à la Jackie O. for the GCA host family dinner party? Absolute perfection. Aunt Tamara's high-heeled Kamali sneakers to the same party? Complete disaster.

✳   ✳   ✳

I was jolted awake. In an attempt to turn the alarm off with my foot, I lost my balance and rolled straight onto the floor. While the alarm clock alternately buzzed and flashed the time, eight o'clock, my brain was flashing its own message. *Urgent: This is not a drill, this is the real thing!*

53

The day you've been dreaming of your entire life has arrived and you've overslept!

As the cobwebs began to clear, the thought of what day this was came into view. The first day of COUTURE WEEK!! Without a moment to waste, I robotically enacted the following:

8:05—Dashed down to the kitchen and chugged a Michel & Augustin energy drink.

8:10—Quick shower, followed by unexpected hint of nerves.

8:20—Pulled out my folder containing a week's worth of invites to the Haute Couture and stared at them in awe.

8:30—Punched the name "Catherine Deneuve" into *Imogenius* and headed for inner sanctum, aka walk-in closet.

8:32—Pulled down vintage YSL hand-me-down from compartment A, level 21. The black chiffon ribbon blouse and cotton superslim cigarette pants were most definitely to-die.

8:45—Affirmation: You have a much better life if you wear impressive clothes.

8:50—A quick dusting of Chanel Be-Bop (to bring my out inner glow) and a wisp of Vanilla Dream lip gloss.

9:01—Checked the week's itinerary, which as it so happened I'd done every day for the last month. Monday: McCartney, McQueen, Lacroix, Lanvin. Tuesday: Viktor & Rolf, Sonia Rykiel, Balenciaga, Louis Vuitton, and so on.

It read like a who's who of the fashion universe, and that wasn't even counting parties! My date book was *so* filled I wondered when I would have time to take care of essentials like eating, sleeping, flirting, IM-ing, camcording, and lip glossing. A million girls would die to be in my shoes. Literally, I thought, admiring the killer silver lamé stilettos I was presently wiggling into.

Toy panted, staring at me. He was anxious to leave.

"And where do you think you're going? We've got to get you ready too, you know." I pulled open my dresser drawer and found, underneath the gobs of undies, the special jeweled-heart-encrusted collar and leash that Aunt Tamara had left for him. I mean, it wasn't bad enough that *I* spoiled him.

"Let's get you brushed first, Toy, and then we'll see how you look in your new collar," I said. "Just one last thing:

You're not fully dressed until you've put a smile on your face." I pulled the corners of his mouth upward, then giggled while Toy happily sniffed and panted away.

With a kiss, he was ready. "There. All done," I said, placing Toy on the bed, where he promptly snuggled into the down coverlet. Then, swooshing back and forth, I checked out my own reflection in the full-length mirror. One never knows when an it girl du jour will walk past you, mid-paparazzi stalking. I'd absolutely die if I were in the background of some random *Teen Vogue* shot looking less than ultrafab.

The door swung open.

"First prize for best runway walk!" Evie cried, sweeping into the room. "I can't believe you're going to the Couture!"

I sat down on the edge of the bed to gather up the last of my stuff when Evie began unexpectedly asking a trillion questions about Dax. I didn't know what to say, and I definitely didn't know how I felt about Dax. I mean, it was way too early to think *anything*. Other than I'm beginning to like being around him.

I was saved when a chorus of "Che gelida manina" from *La Bohème* came wafting through the air, along with the aroma of freshly baked croissants.

"Mmmm. What is that divine aroma?" Evie said, sniffing the air as the rich, yeasty aroma engulfed us.

"Ohmigod, I can't believe what time it is," I said, glancing at the now broken alarm clock. "I'm supposed to pick up Mick at his hotel—in twenty minutes!" I grabbed Evie's sleeve. Toy barked, "Let's go!" And we all zoomed down the spiral staircase.

Leslie was working away in the Dehillerin-outfitted kitchen. How he convinced Aunt Tamara to let him cart in all his restaurant equipment was beyond me. I mean, last summer this was just your basic French kitchen with the obligatory Lacanche enamel stove, acres of counter space, and cabinets. But now every square inch was jammed with some type of blender or mixer or sandwich press.

"Yo," Leslie said, coming out from behind the counter with two perfect café au laits. He must have been up at dawn, judging by the amount of food splayed across the table. His KISS THE CHEF apron covered a red version of yesterday's black tracksuit. I wondered if he had anything besides "Prada" tracksuits in his wardrobe.

"Have a seat," he said, placing a large plate of freshly made croissants in front of us.

Evie—diet or no diet—
began munching.

"So, how are they?"
Leslie asked as Evie nibbled away.
"I have a test in two hours, and I
think I've finally perfected the recipe."

I tore off a corner and popped it into my mouth. "Ohmigod!" I munched ecstatically. "This is fan-freaking-tastic!" I had to admit, Leslie was definitely one-of-a-kind—with his hemipowered blow-dryer (which totally explained his choice of coif), his soft spot for Puccini and Puzo, and now his out-of-this world culinary skills.

"Mmmumf," Evie added, reaching for a third croissant.

Leslie just soaked it all in.

The door buzzed. I took it as my cue to leave.

It was Georges who, each morning, delivered the news-papers, mail, and dry cleaning, and anything else bound for our humble abode.

He was carrying an assortment of packages, papers, and garment bags, and a very big box. Eyeing me somewhat sus-piciously, he handed me a fax.

"Bows, bows, bows!" Georges exclaimed. "This trend refuses to go away."

Apparently I missed the "bows are over" memo.

"For your information, I'm channeling. Think Catherine Deneuve. . . ." (We fashion people utterly revere her.) "*Network*. 1975," I said.

You see, dressing as a character definitely goes a long way toward quelling a girl like *moi*'s awkwardness and insecurities when in public. It's essential to my allure! And not only that, I would never be able to leave the house if I didn't have a "story" in mind. A story being a theme of what to wear. Truth be known, I'm a method fashion fore-caster. Like a method actor, I get into the role 100 percent. I don't just write about it, I live it. Like today, I'll think and dress like Catherine Deneuve, and out I go all full of confidence and certainty. After all, perception is every-thing.

"It was Faye Dunaway. It was 1976. And it was Calvin

Klein. Not Yves Saint Laurent," Evie corrected. I'll bet she's an ace at Clue.

"Details, details," I said. "I've planned this outfit all week."

"It doesn't flatter—" Georges began.

"Flatter! *Imogenius* is flawless—it has to flatter!!"

"It doesn't flatter . . . *your skin tone.*"

"My *what*?" OMG! I'm having an I-can't-believe-I-wore-that moment, I thought, scrounging in my bag for my iPhone to double-check. Tapping a few keys, I realized that Cissy and I had completely forgotten to take skin tone into consideration as a programming option.

Note to self: Send Cissy fierce e-mail re: skin tone for next generation Imogenius *upgrade.*

Despite his proclamation, I decided to risk the mismatch and head out. By now I was late, and Mick was probably going berserk.

I shoved the fax Georges had handed me in my bag, but before I could say *à tout a l'heure,* he waved the morning papers in my face. *"Alors, regarde."*

To appease him, I snatched the paper and began reading. That's when the angel of death swept down. Suddenly the world stopped moving. Evie, Georges, Toy, everything froze in a singular moment of cosmic emptiness. I stood there and stared at the words—just letters on a piece of paper, really, but I couldn't make sense of them. I couldn't get them to form into something comprehensible. I didn't want to. The headline read: QUELLE HORREUR! MODEL STRIKE KO'S COUTURE.

When I regained consciousness, I was lying on the kitchen floor with Evie, Leslie, and Georges hovering over me. I felt just like Dorothy after waking up from her magnificent adventure in Oz. You know, with the three farmhands hovering over her. Even my little dog, Toy, was there. A small pillow was propped under my head, which, BTW, was pounding. I squinted. Georges was fanning me with a newspaper.

"Evie," I squeaked through tear-stung eyes. "What happened?"

"You fainted when you read the news that Couture was cancelled."

"It wasn't a dream?" I croaked. I mean, one minute I'm in a Couture fluffy fairyland cloud, where everything is to-die-for, and the next thing I know, I'm history—discarded like day-old petit four crumbs.

"The paper," I moaned. "Read it to me."

"Are you sure, girlena?" Evie asked.

Georges and Leslie exchanged knowing looks. I hate when people do that.

"Yeah, you might have some kind of relapse or seizure or something," Leslie added.

Georges eyed me dubiously. "As you wish," he said.

"'3 JULY. PARIS, FRANCE. Last night, in a rare demonstration of solidarity, high-fashion models and super-models came together as one, voting to strike, citing growing disputes between the design houses and modeling agencies over talent fees and perks. The no-work vote was passed on the very eve of the anxiously awaited Couture Week.

"'We can no longer survive on the meager fees that dominate the industry,' stated union president and supermodel emeritus Rachelle Desjardins. 'It's just outrageous. These girls are out there every day, walking, changing clothes, and posing. It's exhausting work.'

"'The timing of the strike is entirely strategic, coming at a moment when the entire city is overflowing with anxious guests and patrons from all over the globe, here to view the latest in couture fashion. Fashion houses have already begun canceling shows and parties.

"'It's simply outrageous,' stated Madame Delaforge, one of Paris's most prominent socialites. 'My social calendar is in complete ruins.'

"'At the moment no formal talks have been scheduled between the two factions, but experts tell us that both are scrambling to rectify the situation in the hopes of getting events underway as quickly as possible. One source, however, informed us late last night that both sides remain deadlocked and no solution will be forthcoming anytime soon. 'There are deep philosophical issues at stake here,' he added. 'I wouldn't hold my breath.'"

Aside from experiencing several impulses to scream at the top of my lungs during the reading, I managed to hear the whole article without fainting again or throwing up. I mean, who did these models think they were, anyway? Didn't they know I had a career to build? What was I supposed to do now? Without Couture Week there'd be no fabulously chic trendsters to shoot. They'd flee the city faster than an A-list super-socialette at a Knights of Columbus barbecue. And with nothing to report, there would be no Hautelaw Paris foreign correspondent. Namely *moi*.

"Let them eat cake!" I shouted in despair.

"Shhh!! Do you know what happened the last time a fashion icon uttered those words?!"

"Hey, I don't know what youse're complainin' about," said Leslie. "Couture Week is just an excuse for a bunch of underfed women to parade around in a bunch of expensive clothes. It's all surface, no substance."

"And?" Evie snarled. "Your point is?"

He shrugged. "Just trying to make Imogene here feel better."

"Haven't you ever heard the expression, 'the truth hurts'?" said Evie.

"Well, *mademoiselle*," Georges said, "I must say good-bye to you now." His tone had an air of finality to it.

"Are you going somewhere?"

"*Oui*. My annual summer holiday."

"When are you leaving?"

"Friday morning."

My phone rang. I looked at Evie, who looked back at me, smiling halfheartedly. We both knew exactly who was calling and why. Evie crossed her fingers. I said a silent prayer: *Please, please, please God, please have Spring let me stay in Paris. I know I haven't always been good—I'm sorry I cut in line all those times at the Barneys sample sale and snuck under the tent for the Jock Lord show without a ticket, and I really didn't mean to get Brooke fired when she stole my pictures and sold them to Haute & About. And I'm*

sorry I didn't correct the salesgirl at Hermès when she undercharged me twenty euros, but I promise never to do anything like that again.

I mean, just as I was beginning to enjoy myself, with Paolo Pangs finally subsiding a bit, the thought of leaving Paris *and* BFF, and even Dax, was more than I cared to think about. I tried being brave, but inside I was destroyed. Surprisingly, a tear trickled silently down my cheek. Everyone had been watching me — probably in the hopes of witnessing a nervous breakdown firsthand.

I clicked the talk button on my phone. Having run through a variety of greeting possibilities in my head, I settled on faux cheery.

"Hi, Spring!"

Then without skipping a beat, I blurted out a fashion forecaster's default nervous reflex: the pronouncement of a new trend.

"Fashion flash, denim is dead!" This was followed by a long string of other flimsy fashion forecasting tidbits. Spring listened patiently. I hoped that she would take the bait. She didn't.

"Imogene, this is a most dire situation. We need something really big to replace the slot being held for the Couture."

Everyone was staring at me. Evie was flapping her hands around for information. "What's she saying? What'd she say?" she whispered.

I made a shooing gesture, hoping she'd stop distracting me.

"The news is out, Paris is on the verge of becoming as dead as a pair of stonewashed jeans," Spring said.

I knew denim was dead!

"Well, you can't believe everything the papers say," I stammered. "I mean—"

"I'm not talking about the *papers*, sweetie, I'm talking about the *competition*." I heard the flick of a lighter, followed by a deep inhaling breath. "I'm referring to that *person* who shall not be named!" In Spring-speak, "that person" was her arch-nemesis-slash-sworn-combatant, Winter Tan.

"You know from firsthand experience, dear, that *they* will stop at nothing to outdo us!"

"Yes, but—"

"And I *will not* allow that to happen!"

Evie pinched me. "What's she saying? Can you stay?? Is she letting you stay in Paris?!"

"Shh!" I snarled. "Do you mind?"

"Mind what, dear?"

"Oh, sorry, Spring," I lied, "I was just telling Toy to be quiet." Naturally, I felt like an idiot. Spring ignored it.

"Right now," Spring explained, "I need to have all of my resources working closely in New York. We barely managed to stop Mick from leaving for Paris last night."

"But what about Hautelaw Paris?"

"Well, it *is* unfortunate, but the timing's simply not right. It will have to wait until next year. I'm sorry, dear, but you're needed in New York."

Think, Imogene! Think!

"I *can* get the coverage. . . ."

"Dahling, with all those fabulous people no doubt already making plans to leave Paris, what will there be left to cover?"

I straightened my spine as a smidge of resolve rolled over me. "Listen, Spring, there's something I haven't told you yet. I was saving it as a surprise, but I've been working on something . . . something *really* different. . . ." OMG! Didn't you just make a promise to you-know-who? I felt my cheeks getting hotter by the moment.

"Well, that *is* intriguing," Spring said.

I refuse to risk any firsthand embarrassment by going into the details of everything I said during the rest of the conversation—my concepts, my visions, my artfully contrived . . . well, suffice it to say, I lied my head off. I mean, what was a girl like *moi* to do?

When I finally hung up, Spring had granted me until Friday. *Or else!*

"Finally!" Evie bellowed, when I clicked off with Spring. "So, what happened?"

"She's giving me four days."

"That's fabulous! Anything can happen in four days," Evie said.

If she was right, I had to get busy.

chapter five

I Skull &
Crossbones Paris

date: JULY 6

Things I hate about Paris:
1. The language barrier (duh!)
2. Droppings à la chien (gross!)
3. Petit vs. supersize morning café crèmes (uggh!)
But mostly what I hate about Paris is . . .
4. I'm going to have to leave it if I don't come up with a big
trend story by the end of the day!

❋　　❋　　❋

The phrase "all dressed up with no place to go" was never more relevant. Over the course of the last few days, the trajectory of Couture ecstasy to gloomyville was a straight line. The express train. I felt as dejected as a booted American Idol. I wondered, why do things happen the way they do? What unseen forces govern the wheel of fortune or disasters that come from out of the blue? Ordinarily I subscribe to the motto "When life hands you lemons, make lemonade." I settled instead for a schmeer of Lancôme Pink Lollipop Juicy Gelée.

Unlike the previous mentally disabling three days, I vowed upon awakening to make a conscious effort to get happy. So I consulted my trusty *Imogenius* SoftWear for what to wear when extradition's in the air. In the darkest of hours, I had but one shiny consolation: Neither sleet, nor rain, nor threat of deportation could curb my obsession with Chanel. But instead of a selection of supertight skinny jeans, a baby tee, a frayed-edge jacket, a few well-placed accessories, and the sweetest intertwined double-C flats popping onto the screen, nothing happened. I hit the button again. Still nothing. I shook it, punching in C-H-A-N-E-L manually. I even hit the Daria Werbowy button. But still, nothing.

I decided to deal with it later. I mean, I had other things on my mind now. I was all but resigned to the fact that within forty-eight hours I'd be crossing the Atlantic once again.

To her credit, Spring had been right. Right now there was *no* style story in Paris, because there *was* no style. Anyone with the slightest smidge of it had already evacuated the city. I mean, this was like the biggest diaspora since the Exodus from Egypt. Even the A-list supersocials had departed for an early holiday. Because without a designer to patronize, launch, wear, host, féte, or gossip about, their purpose in life was obsolete. Though unlike the ancients, they didn't leave by foot. Their departure was hastened strictly via Gulfstream V. All that were left in the city were stray cats and Japanese tourists.

But I wanted to stay—no, I *needed* to stay. I still loved Paris.

In the feelings department, I felt more French than ever. To be truly French, one has got to embrace the French mindset, which has its roots in what is commonly referred to as "melancholy."

I mean, going back to NYC would mean complete and utter failure, not to mention having to confront my feelings re: boyfriend angst, and all the other issues that I'm really good at running away from. And it didn't help that every time I passed a flower shop, all I saw were funeral flowers—mine.

Even when I trawled for happy affirmations, none were forthcoming. Finally Evie suggested a simple strategy for what to do:

1) *Trend spot.* (Well, we know that's out.)

2) *Sightsee.* (Been there, done that.)

3) *Buy massive amounts of clothing.*
(Hmm.)

And when all else fails:

4) *Eat.*

Being completely wretched at that point, I began with number 4, vowing to work my way backward up the list to number 3. (The backward thing again.)

So after I gorged myself on a whole Lionel Poilâne round loaf, just out of the oven, I headed for Colette. I have to admit that the sight of models picketing outside caused some initial resentment; however, once I overcame the desire to take their little signs and bash them over the head with them, I couldn't bring myself to cross the picket line. So I moved on, vowing to return a little later on.

At Gaultier, I got bored waiting for the shop to open. I found a nearby bench, where I accidentally woke up the vagrant sitting next to me (it's considered un-chic to wake up the vagrants of Paris). When I missed my neck in attempting a puff of Femme by Lanvin while IM-ing Evie. So I left.

Vuitton's stunning shop on the Champs-Elysées was next. I stood in line as a shopgirl took my order. But to add insult to injury, the Japanese tourists had bought out all the Vuitton in the entire city.

I made my way back to Colette.

"*Parlez-vous* Erin Fetherston?" I asked the shopgirl. She handed me a so adorably chic dress to try on. Yum! If memory serves correctly, it was look No. 137 from the spring/summer look book. (I have a photographic memory going back years. A truer student of fashion never existed.)

The dress had my name all over it. I know that because as I slipped it on, I felt a ping. A single happy molecule had awakened—that is, until the same shopgirl snarked, "I think the dress is too small for you. *Je pense que la robe est trop petite*

pour vous." (*Zhe pens ke la roab eh tro pe teet poor voo.*)

Well, frock you then!! I mentally shrieked. Keep your stinky cheese and rotten food!

I ran outside as fast as my feet would carry me. I was beyond mad at the models, I was mad at Paris. And everything about it! Hyperventilating, I propped myself up against an old tree. All at once I inhaled a passing whiff of Gauloise mixed with the inimitable scent of my own impending doom.

Suddenly the light of salvation shone upon me. I gazed across the street, where I'd spotted an oasis of calm in a sea of confusion: a magazine kiosk. I bolted to the other side of the street, dodging cars, scooters, and baby strollers, and buried myself in the quiet sanctity of *Vogue*. At this point, any version would do. French, American, British, Italian, German . . . even Australian (it was an emergency!). I devoured them all, and prayed that the Marni sheared-chinchilla bathing suit I found myself obsessing over (on page 307) wouldn't show up on any It-Girls du jour and sell out before I figured out a way to buy it.

Unfortunately, headlines and news items about the Paris Couture debacle were everywhere. In a panic, I ran out of the kiosk and found a quiet little park bench to sit on and think. By then it was clear: I had finally run out of options. Tomorrow I would bite the bullet with Spring and start packing.

"Where are you, fate?" I whispered, exhausted from having roamed the streets of Paris in a stupor for one ugly week. I briefly considered dropping in at HLP to see Dax. But I knew how busy he was with the renovations. Despite the fact that Couture was canceled, Spring had asked that Dax carry on fixing up the houseboat.

So I picked my black-and-white Petit Bateau striped self and my Brigitte Bardot black cotton beret from the park bench, along with my dejected psyche, ready for a really good cry, and dragged myself home just as it began to rain. Sideways.

chapter six

All About Yves

date: JULY 7

mood: CURRENTLY CHANNELING

MORTICIA ADDAMS

✳   ✳   ✳

E vie booked her parents' table at La Cour Jardin, in
the courtyard of the Plaza Athénée, for a semifinal *au
revoir*. Like most of Paris, the cafe was empty except
for a nearby phalanx of chicly manicured, bejeweled, and
coiffed regulars—all of whom sat patiently on the laps of
their equally chic owners.

Under ordinary circumstances it would have been beyond
delightful sitting here in the open air, under big red umbrel-
las, surrounded by ivy-carpeted walls filled with little spar-
rows happily chirping away, while fountains trickled serenely
in the background. Unfortunately, from where I was sitting
the noise was practically deafening. Those once endearing
chirps and the constant drip, drip, drip of running water

merely echoed the hotel's emptiness, making the courtyard feel more like a sanctuary for insane birds than a posh eatery.

Evie was oblivious. I mean, she just sat there reading the newspaper. Not that she could read French or anything, but somehow she always managed to glean the good parts. While she had her paper, I had my PowerBook. I had just finished updating my latest "it accessory" aka video blog (*Affirmation: I embrace the new*), starring who else but *moi*, when Evie said, "Hey, check this out! 'Counterfeit Bags Infiltrate Paris.'"

"And?"

"Believe it or not, it's a major crime here."

"Evie, as interesting as that is, I have more important things on my mind right now."

"Sorry." She closed the paper and flagged a nearby waiter, who proceeded to act as if we didn't exist.

"Did you see that? He completely ignored us."

I mean, trend alert: The French ignore. If you don't pass muster in the chic department, you simply don't exist.

"That's okay, I need practice being ignored for the flight back," I said, recalling my recent Air France debacle.

"Hey, it's not over till it's over, girlena. We'll think of something. We always do, right?"

"I guess," I mumbled, unconvinced.

She rummaged around in her *darling* little bag (at least I could still spot *darling*) and pulled out a small tin of Fouquet caramels. I frowned at her. Eating candy before noon made

73

me completely bilious. A passing thought crept in. I wondered if her yo-yo dieting inclinations were once again springing forth.

"What?" Evie snipped as she defiantly popped a caramel into her mouth. "They help me think! And your sitch, girlena, is going to take some major gray cell action!"

After some chewing, and a few low, growling yummy sounds, she proceeded to say, "The first thing you've got to do is pull yourself together. Look at your nails. Your mani looks more *Transylvanian* than *French*, your complexion is sallow, and your hair . . ."

"What's wrong with my hair?"

Instead of a response, she just tsk-tsked me and resumed flagging down the waiter—though I hardly expected a response, knowing what I now know. Okay, so maybe I annoyed him with my bad manicure and bedhead hair.

A grandmotherly voice lilted from across the adjacent table, "Have some more tripe, sweetie."

I craned my neck in the voice's direction. My eyes lingered a bit longer than they should have. Though her outward physical appearance seemed pleasing, there was something amiss. Then I realized: The woman and her little dog were eating off of the same plate. *Eww! Gag! Blech!*

Some people have severe allergic reactions to things such as bee stings, peanuts, or shellfish, as for me, I suffer from seeing good-taste offenders. Unfortunately, anaphylactic shock in the middle of Paris was out of the question. Though with all the chicsters departing the city, it was no surprise to find a good-taste offender in our midst.

"Quite right, darling," she said to her dog, "I'd avoid it if I were you. It was absolutely disgusting, but you must try the *snails*!"

Double *blech*! Even Toy looked a tad queasy (despite his French lineage).

Another waiter appeared. He was well-groomed and semihunky (gorgeous face, teeny bod). But I was too upset to notice. Artistically rolled napkins and menus were tucked into his apron. (Trend alert: It looks like the art of napkin folding is about to make a comeback. Could letter writing be far behind?)

"*Oui, mademoiselle?*" He smiled, took Evie's napkin, and whipped it open with a snap, placing it across her lap. Did he think she was a slob or something? Then he did the same for me.

"I'll have the lobster salad," Evie said, "and another one of these." She held up her empty Flower Power—Evie's new health drink du jour. "They're absolutely addictive."

"*Bien,*" he said, jotting down the order, then to me, "*Et vous, mademoiselle?*"

"*Avez-vous* cyanide?" I groaned.

"*Pardon?*"

"Just ignore her," Evie said, waving the newspaper at him. "She'll have what I'm having."

"*Bien.*" He bowed slightly and disappeared. Evie frowned.

"You know, girlena, I might not be far behind you."

"What do you mean?"

"There's a rumor going around work that Crispin Lamour is thinking about shutting down early for summer holiday. Which means I, and all the seamstresses and workers in the atelier, will be unemployed. And all the dress factories that would normally be working at warp speed by now will be shutting down production as well. And I don't want to hang around Paris all summer by myself," Evie added. "I'd just wind up —"

"Hey there!" an upbeat voice interrupted. From across the courtyard, heading straight for us, was a girl on a cell phone. She was waving at Evie, exuding a "when-they-made-her-they-broke-the-mold" vibe. She clicked off one call and popped into another. She looked like the kind of girl who has had a phone stuck to her head since the time she could talk.

She was speaking English, but her accent was distinctly French, with a dash of mock Texas twang. As she drew nearer, I noticed that perched neatly atop her blazing red hair sat a munchkin-size straw hat. A pair of trademark-worthy schoolgirl braids and razor-sharp bangs swung in iambic pentameter. Her jacket lapels were retrofitted with Mickey Mouse, Minnie Mouse, and Daisy and Donald Duck pins. She was fashion's version of a mixed metaphor. It was only logical that Evie would know her.

When she finished with her call, she said, "Remember me?"

"Mercie! Hi." Evie smiled, then turned to me and said, "Mercie is an intern at Raison d'Etre, the PR firm."

In Paris everyone has a raison d'être. A split-second doubt had me questioning if I'd really found mine.

"Her boss does all the publicity for the House of Lamour," Evie explained.

"Really?"

"You betcha!" Mercie grinned with so much energy I thought she was going to break into a Cactus Cha-Cha.

She paused a moment, took a long hard look at me, and said, "Ah, but you are not American?"

"Yes, I'm American."

"But you are not eternally cheery, nor are you upbeat."

"Oh, she's just upset," Evie intervened. "She thought she'd be spending the summer in Paris with me, being that we're best friends and all, but with things the way they are, she'll probably be going back home sooner than expected."

"Oooh," Mercie said, expressing her sympathy. Then, "Voilà! You need a mission!" she exclaimed with a broad, slightly crooked smile. "I'm sure I can help. Why don't you come up to my office and we can talk before we all have to say good-bye to our wonderful city? I need a mission too. My boss has already gone. If nothing changes, it looks like I'll be working in my parents' linen shop in Lyon for the rest of the summer. No work, no pay. Maybe we can help each other. No?"

She raised a shopping bag and set it on the table. I couldn't help but admire it. It depicted a famous brand of champagne, beautifully illustrated by an equally famous artist.

"This is from the new collection," Mercie said, noticing my interest.

Only in France does an alcoholic beverage merit its own collection.

She stuck her hand inside the bag, pulled out an envelope, and handed it to Evie.

"My company is throwing a party tomorrow night. My boss won't be there, so I'm in charge," she explained. "It will likely be the last event of the season—everyone will be there. And then, poof, they'll be gone."

Evie opened the envelope. The invitation read, "Night of a Thousand Bubbles."

"Y'all will come, *non*? And bring a friend. The more the merrier," she said, smiling.

It was late in the afternoon by the time I got back to the apartment. After lunch, Evie had gone back to work. We took Mercie up on her party invitation and decided we'd ask Gerard and Dax to come along with us.

In the kitchen, Leslie had pinned a note on the fridge explaining that he'd aced his Escoffier workshop exam with a brilliant rendition of the famed thirteen-course North Pole menu (I won't go into detail, but suffice it to say coronet of fennel foie gras and floating baked Alaska—natch—were some of the highlights). The note also explained that he'd gone bowling with some of his school buddies. Meaning: I was free to wallow in misery to my heart's content. So I did what any girl who was about to be booted out of France would do—I ran to my bedroom, collapsed on the bed, and waited for death to come. It didn't. I sort of wanted to call Mom and Dad, but I definitely didn't want to worry them. Besides, I knew they were leaving for San Francisco, for one of Dad's art exhibits. And Lord knows, I didn't want to bog them down with my troubles. So instead I went online to update my video diary and check to see if there had been any new boyfriend applications, now that Paolo had completely abandoned me.

Just as the site's motto, "A place for BFFs," flashed across the screen, my cell phone *and* the doorbell rang simultaneously. The phone was closer.

"Mortuary," I heaved.

"Madre dios!" a familiar Latina voice snipped in a burst of model ego aggro. "Do you have something against answering your doorbell? I've been ringing it for the last five minutes!"

"CAPRICE!"

I tossed the phone on the bed and sped downstairs, overjoyed with the anticipation of seeing my old friend. I swung open the door. There she was—more striking than ever. A genetic lottery winner, Caprice was a gorgeous, raven-haired beauty with an edgy coolness. Though Caprice was not your average licorice-stick model. She was far curvier. No ifs, ands, or *butts* about it. It's been a year since Jock Lord signed her to an exclusive, multiyear contract for his fragrance and ready-to-wear. Since then, he had attained real supermodel status. This, after years of extreme modeling gigs (i.e., skydiving in couture, off-road driving beauty shots, swimming with sharks, runway walking down the side of Rockefeller Plaza via bungee cord—after which, by the way, it took her days to get her center of gravity back). The last time I checked, she was booked until the year 2010.

She had a chic new Versace bag under one arm and her dog in the other. We hugged. She smelled like lilacs.

"Look, Toy," I said, giving Diablo, Caprice's microdog, a little handshake, "your old friend is here too!"

Caprice set Diablo down, and after the necessary sniffs, licks, and some happy panting, he and Toy were best friends again.

We wound up in the kitchen.

"Where are you staying?" I asked, while Caprice raided the refrigerator.

"I'm at the Ritz," she said, her dark eyelashes naturally curling skyward, "but I'm ready to turn around and go home. Unfortunately, my agent insists I stay for the big march. Wow, look at all this stuff!" she added, referring to Leslie's amazing prepared food.

"March?"

"Uh-huh," she said, nibbling a drumstick off the plate of chicken as she closed the refrigerator door. For all her new-found superstardom, Caprice didn't have any of that cooler-than-thou model attitude. "We're picketing all the designer flagship stores. Can you believe it? Models picketing. I should have stayed in L.A."

We spent the next twenty minutes catching up, which consisted mainly of me recounting my sordid tales of woe — Paolo Pangs and all, and my soon-to-be flight back to NYC. Caprice filled me in on her activities over the last few weeks. Namely, being in Los Angeles for pre–pilot season casting calls.

When we'd finished bringing each other up to date, Caprice called Diablo.

"He loves chicken," she told me, peeking under the table. "Diablo!" she called out. "Where did he go?"

I noticed that Toy was gone as well.

"They must be upstairs," I said, walking toward the

staircase that led to the bedrooms. "Toy! Come here, sweetie."

Then I heard a bark. But it wasn't coming from anywhere inside the apartment. The front door was ajar. I must not have closed it all the way after Caprice came in. OMG!

I ran back into the kitchen and yelled, "Caprice, quick. They're gone!" Caprice dropped her chicken bone and together we dashed out the door and zipped down the stairs, passing Evie on her way upstairs.

"Hi, Caprice!" Evie hollered. "Hey! Where are you guys going?"

"To find Diablo!" Caprice yelled. "And Toy!"

Evie doubled back, following us. Once outside, we followed the yips to the garden path, which led to Georges's cottage.

The cottage was painted in the old French gray, which you see a lot of in this section of Paris. Above the double French doors was inscribed the word CONCIERGE. Octagonal shaped, it had two stories and was no more than ten feet wide. The roof was classic French mansard. And all around were potted plants and herbs of every shape and size. I knocked, and we paused a moment, hoping that Georges had seen Toy and Diablo.

"Maybe he's napping," Evie surmised.

"At six p.m.?" Caprice said.

Evie picked up a small pebble and tossed it at the closed window above.

"Evie!" Too late. The pebble hit the large window and fell into the window box full of geraniums beneath it. No one answered.

81

"When did he say he was leaving?"

"Forget Georges, we've got to find Toy and Diablo," Caprice shouted.

After searching the block and asking passersby if they'd perhaps seen them—with no luck—we headed back to Chez Mwah. By then Caprice was in a panic, and so was I.

As we were about to climb the stairs back to the apartment, I noticed a door in the corner underneath the staircase.

"Wait a sec, we didn't check the basement."

Sure enough, the small doorway under the stairs was unlatched and slightly ajar. I opened it. Inside, it was dark.

"I've never been down here," I said nervously.

I pushed the door open and peered in. We gingerly descended the old wooden staircase. A narrow twist of ancient, crumbling stone steps spiraled downward yet again into inky darkness.

"Hello?" I waited. "Toy? Diablo?"

By now the three of us were huddled closely together, leaning forward into the stairwell, listening.

"Where's a light switch?" Caprice whispered.

I felt around, found what was probably an ancient switch, and turned. Nothing.

I carefully crept down the steps, ready to bolt if I saw a shadow or heard a footstep, or a rat, or any number of real or imagined things that would scare the *Chanel* out of me. Evie and Caprice were semi-right behind, meaning they waited at the top, making sure I reached ground level without encountering any ax-swinging psychopaths, before coming down. By the time I hit bottom, I was hyperventilating so much that

I thought I was going to pass out. Fortunately, I was able to rally my senses long enough to grope around like a maniac for the light switch. When the lights popped on, the only thing I found was a greasy workbench, some rusty tools, a prehistoric washing machine, and a fuse box.

"There you two are!" I shouted with relief. Toy and Diablo were sniffing at a wooden door, whimpering. I picked them up just as Caprice and Evie came down the steps, and handed Diablo off to Caprice.

"What a bad boy you are," Caprice cooed gently.

Who could ever admonish these two cuties?

"Hey," Evie said, circling the room, "what's in here?"

She had pushed open the low, rounded wooden door. It led into an antechamber lined with primordial wine racks.

"Oooh!" Caprice gasped.

"Look!" Evie said, blowing dust off the bottles. "Clos Saint-Denis, Coteaux du Layon, Château-Grillet!" Some of the bottles were truly ancient, dating back more than a century.

"My father would freak at this!" Evie said, ogling the vast wine cellar's inventory.

Evie knows all about wine and food. Calling Evie's dad a megastar restaurateur is an understatement. Reservations at any of his restaurants have a waiting list of nearly a year.

"Talk about *The Count of Monte Cristo*," I whispered, nervously inching forward.

"It's spookier. More like *Phantom of the Opera*," Evie said.

"I think it's romantic—like the secret trysting place of

D'Artagnan and Queen Anne's maid or something . . . you know . . . from that movie," Caprice added.

Evie turned her attention back to the wine. "Ohmigod! Chassagne-Montrachet!" Evie grabbed the bottle and pulled. There was a loud *click*, followed by a *whoosh* of musty air escaping. The built-in wine rack swung open silently, revealing a shadowy passageway behind it.

Nobody said a word. We just stood there, staring. A tiny amount of light made its way in. From where I stood, I could just make out the outline of . . .

"AHHHHHHHH!!" I screamed.

"What is it?" Evie shouted.

"I saw someone! Right there!"

Evie reached through the opening and flipped the switch. And what we saw immediately took our breath away.

It wasn't a person after all. It was a dress form. When our eyes adjusted, we realized that what we were looking at was in stark contrast to the preceding outer rooms. We stared at a white glazed-brick circular room with a domed ceiling that was hung with white pendant lights. Above a desk was a wall full of inspirational swipes—cutout magazine pictures, as well as collection sketches and what looked to be 1940s-era photos of clothing details and Hollywood celebrities. Surprisingly, the fabrics and trim swatches were for the most part contemporary.

"Evie! Look at this!" I hollered, smoothing my hands over yards of silk velvet.

"Ohmigod, oh god," Evie chanted, as she riffled through numerous racks of clothing—all seemingly holding nothing that was less than exquisite. "Girlena, check it out!" She was like a kid in a candy store, not knowing what to look at first.

Caprice looked at me. "There are no labels. No names. Nothing to say who the designer was."

"Or *is*," I said.

"Imogene, no one has been in this room for years. Whoever the designer *was* is long gone. *Muerto!* We may never see the likes of this again," Caprice concluded.

I headed for the desk in search of a clue. Amid the stacks of books on technique, from lingerie to lace making, there was a neat collection of fabric swatches in a range of colors and textures, and fat spools of thread and scissors. Piles of photocopies of drawings were in the other corner, along with a sketchbook. The designer's look book! I grabbed it and flipped through the pages, at first out of curiosity for its contents, then in search of a clue as to its owner.

"If I didn't know better, I'd say this was the work of Yves Montrachet," Evie yelled excitedly over the racks between us. "Probably his very last collection."

"Montrachet?!" Caprice and I shouted in unison.

Not only had Yves Montrachet been the most preternaturally talented designer on the planet, he was an iconoclast; a renaissance man who held more than seventy patents on intricate fabric-weaving methods and machine tools, which allowed him to support his fashion design career. He was credited with bringing back a secret medieval weaving craft found only in the Vatican vaults; it is said that even an alchemist couldn't have figured the technique out. Sadly, his undoing came swiftly. After a highly publicized trademark infringement lawsuit against the House of DuPar, the most respected design house in Paris in the nineties, DuPar was fined $500,000 and required to pay a $5,000 fine for every suit made from the plagiarized design. But it was Montrachet who was dropped from the Chambre Syndicale, and banned from showing his collection in Paris. People say that all the legal wranglings ruined Montrachet's nerves and he just couldn't take it anymore. Unfortunately, without any heirs, his untimely death heralded the end of the House of Montrachet.

"Of course, in reality it couldn't be Montrachet," Evie added, "because everyone knows he jumped off the Rock of Gibraltar after the failure of his last collection."

"I've never seen sketches like this," I said, thumbing through a sketchbook in awe.

Evie grabbed the book from me. "The drawings are so precise and elaborately sketched. Every button, tuck, and seam is delineated, like an architect's blueprints—each sketch is an exact guide to a finished garment. Well, *whoever* executed this is or was clearly a master."

Then she went to a rack and pulled off a skirt. "Look at this," she swooned, as she turned a skirt inside out and ogled the garment's construction. "This detailed seam work is impeccable. And it's all made by hand . . . the hand of a genius."

"What a shame," I said, shaking my head.

"He was unique," Evie said. "Montrachet never draped, and he never explained. He said it was all there in his sketches. No questions were necessary—that is, if you were a superb seamstress. His master head seamstress, Hilda, was famous. She could interpret anything he wanted just from his sketch."

"Okay, all that's well and good, but it still doesn't answer the question of whose stuff this is."

Evie bit her lip and sighed.

Caprice folded her arms and heaved.

"I mean, it's a shame nobody will ever see this stuff. If this wasn't an abandoned collection, this person could have been really famous."

All was silent as we pondered not just the mystery designer's gorgeous collection, but his identity as well.

Finally, as her expression morphed from puzzlement to

wonder, Evie said, "Eureka!" A major idea breakthrough was about to emerge.

"This is it!" she cried. "This is your message from the universe, girlena! And it's the answer to all our prayers. Spring will go crazy for this collection. The whole world will."

I had a tinge of foreboding as I intuited one of Evie's harebrained schemes percolating on the front burner.

"Think of it: Spring needs to skirt off the rival competition by coming up with the next big thing, in lieu of Couture, right? All you have to do is convince Spring that you've found it."

"Found what? An abandoned collection?"

"Believe me, you'll be golden after Spring gets a load of the about-to-be hottest, newly discovered designer on the planet. All we have to do is 'borrow' a few pieces," Evie explained, making quotation marks with her fingers. "We might even get some chic model to wear the clothing," she continued, nodding in Caprice's direction, "which you and I will style, just like a real photo shoot. Then you'll send Spring the coverage, along with a copy of the sketchbook and some swatches and swipes. You'll write the reportage, like you always do. And bingo, there's your big Paris story. Which is how you stay in Paris."

"I'll help," Caprice volunteered. "Maybe I can get some friends to help too. We'll model the clothes, like Evie said, no problem."

"Aren't you forgetting something? Like, there's a big

fat model strike going on right now!" I shouted, in the hopes of bringing Evie and Caprice back to reality.

"It's not illegal to wear clothes. We'll be on the picket line, not the runway!" Caprice said.

"Perfect," Evie said. "If the mountain won't come to Muhammad, Muhammad will come to the mountain."

"This is the stupidest idea ever. This stuff isn't ours. What if it belongs to someone in the building? And they come back and find things missing? Then what?"

"As if. The only people in the building are the tenants. Have you gotten a good look at that bunch lately? I mean, get real, girlena!" She laughed.

"Okay, so maybe whoever designed this stuff wants it to be kept a secret. Did you ever think of that? HUH?? And even if we do 'borrow' these things, what if Spring actually *likes* my coverage? What if she wants to know more? I AM NOT DOING THIS!! No way! Impossible."

I was adamant.

"It's either that, or leave Paris. For good. You decide."

"But Evie," I said as they both stared at me, scowling. Who said peer pressure wasn't potent?

"Okay, so let me get this straight. What you're saying is that we create a blisteringly hot, ultrachic, new-on-the-scene albeit potentially nonexistent fashion designer, so that I get to stay in Paris for the summer with you and we can bum around, have fun, pick up boys, shop till we drop, dance, party, and in general, have more fun than we've ever had in our lives. Is that pretty much the idea?"

"You got it." Okay, so maybe Evie was denied some essential vitamin as a child. "Girlena," she said, using her be-calm-because-I'm-the-voice-of-reason voice. "Trust me. Have I ever steered you wrong?"

"Do I have to answer that?"

Late that afternoon, I took a package marked URGENT to the FedEx office. This would prove to be my first fatal mistake. Little did I know that I was about to become the most Googled fashion-forecasting intern on the planet.

chapter seven

"*Faaaabulous*!!!"

date: JULY 8

mood: CURRENTLY CHANNELING
JACKIE O. ON SKORPIOS — WHITE
JEANS, JACK ROGERS SANDALS,
BLACK SILK SHIRT, HERMÉS SCARF,
AND VERY, VERY DARK GLASSES.

✳   ✳   ✳

sailed into the office at noon, expecting Spring's phone call. Instead I found a shirtless Dax on deck, applying a coat of Schiaparelli pink paint — thicker than marshmallow frosting — to the houseboat's exterior. Normally that particular color (and its applicator) would have lifted my spirits; however, having spent last night in a state of unmitigated wretchedness over the hastily assembled package and its possible rejection and/or acceptance by said employer, all I could do was fake a smile. I waved and went inside.

The phones were still not connected, and I'd hoped that

Spring would completely space on my cell number. Just to make sure, I'd accidentally hit the off button. (Oops.) Anyway, while I mulled over a zillion potential excuses to give Spring, Dax appeared in the doorway with *his* cell phone.

"*Pour toi,*" he said with a smile, offering his phone to me.

"*Merci,*" I replied. "Hello?" I mewed into the phone.

To my profound relief, Spring bellowed fashion's favorite adjective: "FAAAABULOUS!!!"

I was saved.

"Dahling. Your package was divine. *How ever* did you find him?!"

I said a silent thank-you to the universe.

"The snapshots, genius!! The sketches, brilliant! The look book, the samples . . . there are no words!!"

"Thank you, Spring," I replied, trying to sound as humble as possible while my knees buckled.

"But, my dear," Spring continued, "you forgot one teensy little detail."

"Detail?" I said lightly.

"Yes. You forgot to include the designer's name, dear."

OMG. In the rush, it hadn't occurred to me that he needed a name.

"Imogene, are you there?"

"Name? Name. Oh right, name. He um, he goes by the name of . . . nobody!"

"Nobody?!"

"What I mean is, he doesn't have a name. I mean, of course he has a name." I laughed nervously. "That is, um . . .

well, truth be known, it's a *veeeeeery* hard name to pronounce. Ummm . . ."

"Sweetie, not that it matters, under the circumstances, but overseas calls are a fortune these days."

I desperately scanned the room for something with a name on it, but Dax had cleared the room out completely. The only thing left was and old calendar tacked to the wall, the days crossed off with big red *X*s.

"X!" I shouted. Although I knew that this person without appropriate nomenclature had to have a proper name, X was the best that I could come up with at that moment.

"Mr. X?!"

"Well, being French, he calls himself Monsieur X." (Pronounced *eeks*.)

"What kind of name is *Monsieur Eeks*?!"

"Oh, that's just his stage name."

"He's in the theater?"

When it comes to unsubstantiated rumors, the fashion scene is worse than the weekly gossip magazines. It was my job to set the record straight—even if it was a tad inaccurate.

"Oh yes, I mean no . . . it's just that he's beyond names. After all, they are a tad last millennium," I said with a laugh. "It's just that he's, uh, extremely shy, and well, basically, he . . . um . . . prefers to remain anonymous."

"And how do we reach this Monsieur Eeks?" Spring asked.

"Actually, you'll probably find this pretty funny, Spring, but I'm his sole contact."

"Really?" Spring said slyly.

"He doesn't want anybody to know who he is. Except for me, of course. And he doesn't want anyone to know *anything* about him," I added. "He's only doing it for the sake of his art."

"Art for art's sake. I love it! It's so French!"

I knew Spring's eyes were twinkling.

"He is French, is he not?"

"*Very* French!" I confirmed.

"Hold on a minute, would you?" Spring interrupted.

"Malcolm!" Spring held her hand over the receiver. I heard her muffled voice in the background. "I'm waiting five minutes already for my Kabbalahtini, dear!!" Then back to me she said, "So what you're saying is, that is, if I understand you correctly, this is an *exclusive*?"

"Um, exclusive . . . yes! Totally exclusive!"

"Listen, dear, I want you to send me more. More sketches, more samples. Anything you can get your hands on. Can you do that, dear?"

"I'll try."

"There is no *trying*, there is only doing."

What Spring meant was, just make sure I lock Monsieur X up before Winter Tan makes a play for him.

"Now off you go, dear. I don't want to hold you up unnecessarily. Besides, I have many phone calls to make," Spring said with a loud, relishing slurp followed by an extra-long drag from her cigarette. When she spoke again it was in a decidedly more relaxed tone.

"Imogene, sweetie," she purred. "You've made me unimaginably happy."

Okay, so Spring was a little more enthusiastic than I had planned. But that was good, right? After all, fashion forecasting was, to put it mildly, a tad past its heyday. Spring had always looked for new ways to "grow" her business. I guess as something of a futurist, she looked into her crystal ball one day (literally) and saw the writing on the wall. Fashion forecasting had new competition, and not just from other fashion forecasters. Blogs, instant runway coverage from a plethora of websites, and other sources were springing up each day, encroaching little by little on Spring's turf. Spring knew she had to expand her business or it would ultimately die.

Back at the apartment that afternoon, I was ready to execute part *deux* of the stay-in-Paris-no-matter-what plan. We agreed that Caprice and some model friends would in fact wear some of the pieces we'd found in the atelier while picketing. I would, camcorder in hand, just so happen to be swinging by at that precise moment, shoot the coverage, and send it to Spring. And since Paris was as dead as last season's Balenciaga bag, most of the media had already fled town, so there wouldn't be any other press coverage to worry about. In the final analysis, I guess the plan was beyond genius.

After I was sure that Leslie was nowhere to be found (it was potluck dinner Saturday, a weekly advanced gastronomic get-together he had with his school buddies, and he was never home before midnight), I snuck downstairs to the hidden atelier.

Evie had already selected a rack full of clothing for the models. All that was left to do were a few basic fittings.

Caprice and a couple of model friends were there. I found Evie on one knee, pins in mouth as she gathered the hem on one of the models, who looked (and acted) as if she were just out of braces and pigtails. Actually, I recognized her. She was the model Crispin Lamour wrapped in plastic wrap and stuck inside his NYC shop window for twelve hours last December. I heard she lost ten pounds and thanked him by having a ghostwriter pen a book about the experience.

When Evie had finished, she stood up and considered her work. The model walked around the room, then came back and stopped in front of Evie, who made a final adjustment.

"Okay, let's go over this one more time," Caprice said. "We'll all meet here at nine thirty tomorrow morning."

"Nine thirty?!" the other model, Araminta (Minty, for short), protested. Then she flipped her honey blond hair into a ponytail and reluctantly slipped out of her skinny JBrand jeans for her fitting.

"My eyes don't like, even open until eleven," said Ferebee, a brunette model.

"Mine, like, don't open until one," Minty added.

"By the way, girls, whatever you do, *please* don't mention any of this to anyone. Not the clothing, not the fitting, nothing. Okay?"

"Secrets, yay! I just loooove secrets!" Minty chirped.

"Me too!" added Ferebee.

"No, really," I said, trying not to sound too desperate, "nobody can know. *Nobody.*"

"My lips are, like, sealed," Ferebee quipped, pretending to zip her lips.

"My lips are, like, glossed!" said Minty, and the two of them went off into peals of laughter.

Caprice cleared her throat loudly—obviously in need of a change of subject. "The strike, ladies, begins at ten," she said flatly.

"Strike?" Ferebee said. "I thought we were picketing."

I fought an overwhelming urge to roll my eyes.

"The bus will pick us up here at nine forty-five sharp," Caprice said.

"Bus" really wasn't the right word. It was more like one of those ultradeluxe, no-holds-barred land yachts, packed with dressing rooms and bristling with decadent perks like satellite TV, champagne by the magnum, and caviar. A group of rogue stylists calling themselves Coup de Coif had formed out of sympathy for the allegedly beleaguered models. They volunteered to do the hair and makeup for the day. Protests were scheduled to happen at several locations around the city, so the land yacht was hired to shuttle them around in splendor.

"I need some, like, music," said Minty, who started moving in that you-know-my-body's-perfect way. "How am I supposed to get centered without my music?"

"And how am I supposed to get centered without something bubbly?" added Ferebee.

"This is just a fitting." I sighed with an air of annoyance. If I were Evie right now, I'd be sticking pins into Ferebee instead of the swath of crepe black satin she was pinning over her shoulder.

Evie swatted a stray hair off her forehead and stepped back to check her handiwork.

"There's something missing," she mused. While the models were busy marveling at themselves in the mirror, Evie stood there scrutinizing the pieces Ferebee and Minty were wearing. "It needs something." She took a step back and looked at the dresses. "It's the fabric."

"I thought we were just 'borrowing' a few pieces. Not *redesigning them.*"

"Maybe through here," she said, pointing to the bodice and totally ignoring my comment. After some serious perusal, she snapped her fingers and said, "I have a piece of lace upstairs that would be absolutely perfect."

"I'll get it," I offered.

"That's okay, you won't know which one I mean. I think Georges put it in the closet. It's probably buried under a ton of other stuff."

We went upstairs together. The foyer closet was jammed with every kind of box imaginable.

"It's the one on the bottom of the top shelf . . . there"— Evie pointed—"under those bolts of fabric. The ones with the teetering box way on top."

I stretched as far as I could, managing to get my hand clamped around the bolt of fabric covered in brown paper that Evie was pointing at. I yanked lightly, desperately trying not to bring down the entire pile. After a few unsuccessful tugs my hand began to cramp, followed by my legs, followed by my tiptoes, so I gave the bolt a good yank. I mean, it wasn't *quite* like an avalanche, not that I've ever been in one, but everything did rush out at once, knocking me back into Evie.

When we had recovered, Evie shouted, "Ohmigod! Look!"

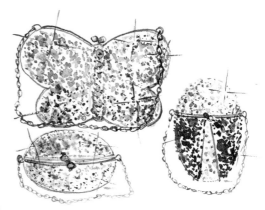

The teetering box had popped open, and a cache of jewel-encrusted bags had spilled out across the parquet floor, all twinkling with an assortment of gold, platinum, and chunky colored stones. Some were shaped as animals and bugs; others were reminiscent of Faberge eggs.

"Wow," Evie yelped, grabbing the nearest bag. "These are the nicest Austrian crystals I've ever seen," she said, inspecting the bag in the shape of a butterfly.

I picked one up that looked just like Toy. "Oooh, a French bulldog puppy!"

"To-die," Evie said.

I flipped the box over and there, in big red letters, was the word "Pacojet."

"Ohmigod! Evie!! This is the box!"

"What box?"

"The box Leslie picked up at the warehouse the day I flew in! Remember I told you?"

"And?"

"These bags are counterfeit!" I whispered in horror. "You know? Like in the paper!"

"Leslie?!"

"Of course Leslie, who else? He must be one of those bag counterfeiters. Why else would he have a box full of them?"

"I don't know," Evie said, "maybe he buys in bulk."

"There are no Costcos in France, Evie! He's probably selling them."

"Maybe we can get a discount. . . ."

"Evie!"

"Look, girlena, you're jumping to conclusions. You don't even know if they *are* counterfeit."

"And if they aren't, it means he stole them. He's probably not even enrolled at Le Cordon Bleu — it's probably just a front!"

"Okay, so what do we do? Call the cops?"

I didn't know what to do.

"Actually," Evie continued, with a cunning smile curling around her lips, "they match the evening dresses perfectly."

"Isn't bling a tad over?" I said, hoping she wasn't going to get any weird ideas about using the bags, too.

"Bling is about to be reborn!"

Unfortunately, like any fashion trend, what goes around comes back around — eventually.

"So," Evie said, "whaddya think?"

It was tempting. If I could suspend my disbelief that these were in fact counterfeit bags, I could imagine how much more gorgeous the collection would look accessorized with them. My inner voice — you know, the one that always wants you to do things you know you shouldn't, the things that almost never work out for the best — pondered the situation.

"We'll just sort of, like, borrow a few bags for the shoot," Evie said, piling an assortment onto her lap. "We can sneak them back right after, just like we're doing with the collection. No one will ever know."

Did I mention my inner voice sounds a lot like Evie?

Later that evening, per Mercie's invitation, Evie and I entered the restaurant where her Night of a Thousand Bubbles fete was already underway. Evie took more care than usual in dressing for the party. Since meeting Gerard, her style was morphing a tad. Ordinarily on a night like this, Evie's look might run a hair on the gothy side. But of late, she'd been tapping more and more into her inner *femme*. She actually looked quite beautiful in the midnight blue cocktail dress—a little number dating from her Rita Hayworth series a couple of years back. (Evie was the queen of DIY.) And for the first time in years, her hair was actually styled, as opposed to the Medusa-like hair extensions she up till recently sported. And her little tiara was darling. She glowed in a way I'd never seen before.

As for *moi*, in choosing an alter ego for the evening, I'd narrowed the choices down to three: the Bombshell, the Cutie, the Sophisticate. Since Evie was going the Starlet route, I, flashing my faux-glowing legs under a wispy, pale pink chiffon Marchesa baby-doll dress, opted for the Cutie, which offered just the confidence boost a girl such as *moi* required while entering a party with only her BFF.

We sauntered through the candlelit restaurant. Its red walls, velvet banquettes, and sultry lighting oozed haute bordello. I scoped out the room at once to see if Dax had arrived yet. Evie did the same regarding Gerard.

In the distance, a mini disc jockey setup spun French hip-hop while the few remaining members of the A-list Parisian party circuit mingled, nibbled, and sipped signature champagne next to a larger-than-life-size ice sculpture of the three kings of culture: Lacroix, Lagerfeld, and Lamour.

Despite my trepidation about tomorrow, I snatched an hors d'oeuvre from a passing waiter's tray. I hoped desperately that all would go well.

But that wasn't the only thing. The question of the counterfeit bags weighed heavily on my mind. I was confused. After all, we were merely borrowing them.

I was probably being silly, thinking Leslie could possibly be mixed up with a criminal counterfeiting ring. No way. But if he were, well shouldn't we be calling the police? Then again, there's that teensy little issue of tomorrow's photo shoot . . .

As we made our way through little clusters of cliques in search of Mercie, a pale passing waif distracted me from my thoughts. She blew a gale-force wind of France's version of air pollution — secondhand smoke — in our direction. More than a tad *l'anorexique*, she wore a T-shirt that read MAKE LOVE, NOT FASHION (eeww) and a pair of H&M castoffs. She stomped her cigarette into the ashtray on a nearby table and gave my shoes a stare.

In a burst of unbridled shoe-gasm, she pointed at my feet and shrieked, "Where did you get those? I have been looking everywhere for them. I loooooove them!"

I made a mental note (considering the source): *Donate shoes to local French charity qfh (quick, fast, and in a hurry),* then hurried off toward a grouping of tables, in hopes of finding more civilized companionship.

When we'd successfully lost the shoe freak, Evie mused, "It's so romantic here. This would be a great make-out place."

"Not that you would know," I said, implying her lack of devotion to anything but a needle and thread.

"What do you mean by that?" she sputtered. "For your information, I have an admirer. And his name is Gerard. Remember?" Before she had a chance to elaborate, my heart skipped at least a beat. Karl Lagerfeld had just sashayed into the restaurant. He was accompanied by an entourage including a butler, who walked beside him carrying nothing but a bottle of Pepsi Max. They were immediately escorted to a nearby reserved table.

"Evie. Look!" I said, pinching her arm.

Evie followed my eyes and chuckled. "That's not the real Lagerfeld. It's his stand-in."

"What do you mean, not real?"

"Fakes. Stand-ins," she said, impervious to my dismay.

It seemed that a *real* trend was brewing in Paris this summer after all, albeit a very subtle one: celebrity look-alikes.

As I turned to catch one last glimpse of the faux Lagerfeld, I noticed Gerard standing in the doorway, scanning the crowd for Evie. He was a tad on the short side, and his thick, rectangular glasses gave him an arty vibe. Dax was with him too — looking every bit adorable. He wore a loose-fitting black suit, a tie, and the surprise of vintage white Reeboks. In his hand, he held a single pink rose. His hair was messed up in the cutest way, and with his smile and sun-kissed skin, he radiated *Ooh la la!*

"Gerard!" Evie shouted in a girlish swoon upon spotting him. Her eyes twinkled.

As they approached, Evie asked, "Do I look all right?" Now I saw why she'd been a tad beyond distracted lately: She'd gone MENtal!

"You look wonderful." (I'm nothing if not supportive.)

I think she'd finally found the ultimate diet: a hot crush.

"What do you think, girlene?" Evie whispered to me as he approached.

Her happiness meant the world to me. "I think you're smitten!"

She smiled a crazy, goofball grin, beaming brightly enough to power a small town in Alaska.

"I know he's not overtly gorgeous, but he has other things going for him."

"Evie!" I admonished. "I think he's absolutely adorable." There was a brief pause, and then I asked, "Like what?"

"He knits." Having obviously observed the quizzical look on my face, she added, "And he sews." That's all she had to say. It was a match made in heaven.

As soon as Dax spotted me, he smiled a big, bright white smile. I tingled all over, surprising myself at how happy I was to see him. He waved, slicing his way effortlessly through the scant crowd.

"Now *he's* adorable!" Evie gushed.

Yes, he was, I thought.

When Dax reached us, he dropped a big, sweet double

dollop of kisses across my cheeks and said flirtatiously, "*Chérie*, you look adorable tonight."

Of course, I blushed to my toes. Without missing a beat, I repuffed my sheer sleeves (which had just the right degree of transparency without looking vulgar), fluttered a faux row of full black Swarovski-studded lashes, and flirted back with, "Did you know that fennel grows on the North Pole?"

Hello, news flash, I thought as a twinge of guilt touched down on my conscience, flirting *sooo* equals cheating. I cautioned myself. I knew I was getting a bit caught up in Dax. How could I not? Why should I not? I mean, you can't help it if in Paris you just fall in love in the blink of an eye. And Dax was so sweet, and he was beyond adorable. But despite all that, I knew deep down that I still had feelings for Paolo. Despite the *Priscilla thing*.

"Would you like drinks?" Gerard asked us.

"We'll have two Shirley Temples," I said.

I've taken it upon myself to reinvigorate one of the oldest nonalcoholic retro-girl drinks in history. I think it's perfectly ginchy to order one, so go ahead and do the same the next time you're faced with this quandary. Everyone will think you're beyond chic. Who knows, you might even start your own trend.

I called after Dax, "And don't forget the cherries!"

"I'll help Dax," Gerard said to Evie with a smile.

"I'll be waiting." Evie winked flirtatiously. Gerard

seemed to hang a minute on her smile, until Dax tapped his arm.

Evie and I had just settled into an overstuffed banquette when a universal gasp suddenly filled the room. Evie had second thoughts and decided to help Gerard with their drinks.

All heads turned toward the entrance. Caprice had arrived with Ferebee and Minty, looking drop-dead gorgeous.

Caprice was ultrahot. Clouds of hair tumbled past her shoulders, gleaming like a bolt of cocoa-colored silk charmeuse. Her essence rendered every other female's estrogen powerless. She waved a wrist full of cognac diamond stackables in the air and flashed her lash extensions coquettishly over her shoulder, achieving the desired effect. Cameras flashed and cell phones flew out of designer bags faster than panties at a Tom Jones concert. Before you could say "And God Created Woman," Caprice was surrounded by a bevy of admirers. After all, beauty is the most potent social currency in the world.

"Caprice!" I shouted. "Over here!"

A minute later she flopped down next to me, while her model friends floated off. A waiter miraculously appeared. Hanging with Caprice had its obvious advantages. We helped ourselves to his tray—I grabbed a Pimms gelée with raspberries and fromage blanc, while Caprice snapped up what looked like crab salad with lemon verbena gelée. Yum!

After some initial chitchat, Evie returned with Gerard and Dax—and Mercie.

Evie said a quick hello to Caprice and made a few introductions all around, then turned to me. "Do you see Minty and Ferebee talking to that guy?"

"So?"

"So, I think it's time for a little girlo-a-girlo chat with Ferebee and Minty. I ear-witnessed them telling him all about Monsieur X!"

"What?!" Caprice and I stood up in unison.

"See that preppy guy with the black horn-rimmed glasses?" Evie said.

"That's Olivier DeDompierre, from *Maven Magazine Daily*," (more commonly known as *MMD*) Mercie said. Preppy was wearing a green Lacoste shirt, pink slacks, a rainbow-striped belt, and loafers—no socks. Sweeping his blond hair off his forehead with a quick snap of the neck, he appeared to be listening very attentively.

"He's a notorious gossip. He's the reason Jock Lord and Karenna Rosenfield are feuding. Not such a great fact-checker," Mercie said, shaking her head. "Only who's that with him, I wonder?"

I swung back around to see who Mercie was referring to. OMG!

"It's Brooke!" I shuddered.

"*Sans* the Wolfe Pack!" Evie added.

"What's she doing here?"

"She smells *Eau de Scoop*, that's what she's doing here!" Evie said. "Brooke's the one we should worry about Minty and Ferebee spilling the beans to. And if Winter Tan and Spring are both vying for Monsieur X, it's bound to get ugly."

"Wait here," I said.

With no plan whatsoever, I jumped up and slinked across the room, as casually as someone on the verge of committing hara-kiri *can* slink, keeping myself well hidden from Brooke. She was standing by herself—that is, without another Wolfe Pack member in sight. I mean, what in the world were Minty and Ferebee telling her and that reporter? All I knew was that Evie was right. If Brooke found out, it would set off a nuclear fashion war. I'd suffer more firsthand embarrassment than the time Jenna Evans came to school after Christmas break with last year's cell phone. Poor thing—why don't parents get it? Not to mention the fact that faster than you could say Betamax, I'd be history.

I continued moving toward them. Fortunately, I was able to maneuver myself behind the only other people in the vicinity. My cover was a handsome Spaniard in a silver Armani suit and an überslender, gothlike woman. (Trends rise and fall, but there are some crazes that, despite the best efforts of designers to ditch them, the public won't relinquish.)

I couldn't quite overhear what Minty was saying but did manage to catch a "Really?" and one or two "Uh-huhs" from Preppy Man before skooching closer for better audio quality. By this time I had infiltrated their inner circle, shielded from them all by the Spaniard. Goth Woman sucked her cheeks in and scowled at me—a small price to pay to hear Minty completely run off at the mouth.

"Do we know you?" she purred in a sultry German accent.

"Did you notice how when the light catches this ice sculpture just so, the figure looks a lot like Barry Manilow?"

While they were trying to figure that out, I inched closer to Minty. "And nobody knows about him," she said. "He's like, completely undiscovered."

"His name is Monsieur X? Funny," Preppy Man said.

"You can't tell *anybody*, because it's, like, a secret," Ferebee added.

"Don't you just loooove secrets?'" said Minty.

"I won't say a word," Preppy Man assured them with a devilish smile.

"You can count on me," added Brooke.

"You know, *señorita*, I believe you are correct," the Spaniard replied thoughtfully. "I believe that is Barry Manilow."

I glanced at the statue, and when I turned back, Brooke was gone.

Just then, Minty turned and caught my gaze. I waved for her to come over, but clearly she wasn't getting it.

"Oh, look, Minty! It's Imogene!"

"Imogene! What are you doing here?!" Minty asked with genuine surprise.

Ferebee turned and whispered something to Preppy Man. He studied me carefully.

I silently recited some inner peace mantra I had read on a box of organic oat flakes. Then I flashed as many teeth as I could muster under the circumstances.

"Minty! Ferebee! What a surprise!" I chirped, a little too eagerly for anyone who was paying attention. "Can I speak to you two for just a teensy second?"

I looped my arms into theirs and steered them out of range of Preppy Man.

"I'm detecting, like, an aura of tenseness here," Ferebee said.

"Yeah, like, really stressed out," added Minty.

"What are you guys *doing*?!" I hissed under my breath.

"Just talking to some guy."

"Who?"

"How should we know? It's not like there are a lot of people here to talk to. Besides, he's, like, practically the only *man* at the party."

"Yeah," Ferebee added. "Except for the statue of Barry Manilow."

"Who's Barry Manilow?" wondered Minty.

"Forget Barry Manilow! You're not supposed to be talking about Monsieur X!" I cried.

"Why ever not?"

"Because it's a secret!"

"And?" Minty asked.

"Yeah, like, and?" Ferebee echoed. "I mean, like, what good is a secret if you can't tell anybody?"

"But we talked about this at the fitting. Remember when I asked you to please not mention—"

"At the fitting?" Ferebee rolled her eyes. "You can't expect us to remember that far back."

It was then that I realized there was no point in going further. The damage was done. When I looked back at the ice statue, Preppy Man was gone, which meant all I could do now was hope he shared the same short-term memory issues as Ferebee and Minty. Because Brooke certainly didn't.

"Hello, Imogene."

Speak of the devil. I did a one-eighty. Brooke was standing right behind me.

"Brooke. What are you doing here?" I asked innocently.

As usual, she was dressed to kill. In fact, she'd make a perfect Bond girl. The evil one. I mean, I hated to admit it, but if you didn't know her you'd think that she was quite beautiful. She had a full mane of blond hair. She was taller than me and had a gorgeous figure. Her designer of choice tonight was Versace. Head to toe.

"Listen, lame-o. I know what's going on here. You think you're so great. You think you got lucky, don't you? Well, guess what, I know all about Monsieur X. And I know that you don't have a clue as to where he is or how to find him. Well, here's a news flash. You can stop looking, because I'm the one who's going to find him first — not you! With Winter Tan's foot soldiers all over Paris, Spring doesn't stand a chance with just little old you, so why not quit while you're ahead?"

She really didn't have to try hard; Brooke knew how to rattle my cage.

But what Ferebee and Minty didn't know, and more important, what Brooke and Preppy Man didn't know, was not only did I not know Monsieur X's identity, but he was potentially nonexistent.

The last thing I needed right now was Brooke's interference.

chapter eight

I Skull & Crossbones Paris Part Deux

date: JULY 9

Attention, universe. I have a question. How does one know whether a problem is a warning or a test? I felt the emergence of a new affirmation: When in doubt, pout!

❋   ❋   ❋

Despite the fact that Brooke was threatening to throw a monkey wrench into our plan, she really knew nothing. I mean, what was I getting all worked up about, anyway? With today's simple plans, what could possibly go wrong? By the time we shoot the clothes, I'll be on to the next stage. No one will be any the wiser. Besides, I have no doubt that soon the strike will be all settled and forgotten and no one will remember anything about it. And all traces of Monsieur X will fade away with the next hot thing. If not, well, this was a big city. How fast could a secret seep out?

After a quick *petit déjeuner* of Red Bull and sushi (Caution: This is what happens when you hang with models), I went to work.

Caprice was a real champ, showing up with the retention-challenged twins, Ferebee and Minty, in plenty of time for the land yacht. Evie, likewise, was ready with two full racks of scrumptiousness, and I, for my part, had done a preshoot check of batteries, memory sticks, camera, and camcorder. Unfortunately, as the land yacht was about to set sail for the Avenue Montaigne, I realized I'd forgotten the jeweled bags for the shoot.

I told Evie I'd follow by car, waved my *bon voyages*, and scampered upstairs to grab the contraband. I took my time and leisurely logged into my e-mail. I mean, they still had to do hair and makeup, so there was no rush. There were a bunch of e-mails in my in-box. One caught my eye for its absence. (Guess who?) But by now, while still a bit unsettled, I had begun getting used to the idea that in the grand scheme of things, Paolo might have more to do with my past than my future.

The e-mail that did catch my eye, and the only one I had time to open, was from Cissy. The others would have to wait. It was marked URGENT.

> To: Imogene
> Fr: Cissy
> Re: *Imogenius*
> I hate to be a buzz-killer, but of late I've been dealing
> with some minor problems. A few girls have requested
> refunds, claiming our *Imogenius* SoftWear is buggy.
> Unfortunately, the family vacation started, like,
> yesterday, so I've given everyone your e-mail address
> in case any further problems arise.
> TTFN!

I took the Alexander III Bridge (Neptune gazing down on me from the top of the bridge always gave me goose bumps). I zoomed down the Cours Albert 1er to Rue François 1er. With most of Paris on vacation, and it being Sunday, the drive over was a breeze. That is, until I hit Avenue Montaigne. To my surprise, as I rounded the corner I hit a sea of bleating horns and irate cab drivers. At first I thought there was an accident, but as I slowly weaved my way through traffic, past a few curious pedestrians and near-empty tour buses, I began to realize that the source of confusion was coming from somewhere near the center of the block.

I don't really remember when my stomach began to twist into knots. Certainly not when I passed the first news truck

114

(it was local). There was bound to be some small interest in a group of picketing models (if that's what it was). Perhaps it was when I passed the second, or third, or fourth news truck (this one from CNN). But when I saw the land yacht, anchored amidst an ocean of cheering people, my stomach began doing Olympic-quality somersaults.

The crowd was in a complete uproar. People cheered and applauded while camera flashes popped faster than champagne corks on New Year's Eve. I found a teensy parking spot next to a news van, gathered up a couple of the bogus bags that had spread across the passenger seat, and slammed the door, pushing my way into the teeming masses. From that distance I could only hear what sounded like a bunch of PMS-stricken Greenwich High School cheerleaders on a rampage:

"No way! No way! We can't live on ten grand a day!"

I couldn't squeeze forward any farther so I went vertical, climbing onto the hood of an old Renault. From where I was perched, I could see the entire media circus in full and horrific bloom.

To my left, a line of licorice sticks, dressed in to-die-for Monsieur X, paraded the length of the storefront one at a time—catwalk style. Wow! They must have taken it upon themselves to stage their picketing like a runway show. One model would leave the land yacht, prance around the picket line in a circle, and return to the land yacht for a change. Each new change would evoke a gasp of delight from the crowd. And each model brandished a tiny picket sign, tastefully mounted on the end of a slender, black enameled stick, proclaiming sayings like: NO FREEBIES! NO FAIR! and I WON'T GET OUT OF BED FOR LESS THAN $25,000 A DAY.

I froze in disbelief. I mean, it was one of those moments when everything suddenly moves in slow motion. You know, as if the world was plunged underwater and all you could do was stare, slack-jawed.

I tried calling Evie on my cell phone, but I couldn't reach her. After that, all I remember is standing there on the hood of the Renault, unable to move, watching Ferebee, Minty, and the others give their show while an army of journalists went absolutely berserk. The moment didn't end. It just went on and on like some hazy dream that slowly plays out in an endless loop of misery.

Then someone screamed at me.

"Heeeeeey!"

I closed my mouth and looked down. Someone was standing next to the Renault, gaping up at me. That someone cupped their hands around their mouth and hollered again.

"Girlena!! What are you doing?!"

Slow motion reverted to normal speed.

"Evie!" I yelled over the pandemonium. "What happened? Where did all these people come from?"

She yelled something back, but it was lost in the uproar. I climbed down from the car.

"When we got here everything was fine," Evie said. "I mean, nobody was here. Then all these news trucks swooped down on us out of nowhere."

I looked over at Ferebee and Minty, who were now talking to reporters. Evie followed my gaze.

"I tried to stop them, but they wouldn't listen!" she hollered.

"Where's Caprice?"

Evie shook her head and shrugged. "In the trailer, last time I looked."

"We've got to shut them up!" I shouted. Squeezing, elbowing, prodding, jostling, and generally pushing and shoving, we made our way toward the land yacht. We wound up crammed behind the front line of reporters, who were gawking at Minty as she blathered about everything she could think of (which actually wasn't much). To her credit, though, she looked *incredible*, and the clothes were even more beautiful in daylight—if that was possible.

"It's such a drag being on strike," Minty continued. "I mean, like, standing outside all day with no driver and no personal assistants. And, like a ginormous lack of, like, freebie clothes and bags and shoes? Like, how do they expect us to live on so little? Have you checked gasoline prices lately?"

She stopped to breathe and the reporters jumped, shouting over one another. That's when my worst fears were confirmed. The reporters weren't interested in Minty or Ferebee or anything remotely associated with the model strike. There was only one thing they wanted to know about.

"Who made your dress?"

"What is the name of the designer?"

The girls didn't seem the least upset that the questions didn't concern them personally—they just wanted to be in front of the camera. But then, models can't really help themselves. They're born with a natural *amour* for cameras—

sort of a sixth sense. They continued smiling, tilting their heads and shoulders to the camera so their hips stuck out, assuming the classic model pose. A blinding display of camera flashes ensued.

"Who is this couture genius?"

"Oh, this?" Ferebee asked, pouting her lips and pushing her shoulder to her chin. "Well, there's, like, this mysterious designer."

"And all we know about him," Minty added, "is that he doesn't have a name."

"Yeah, like, they just call him Monsieur X!"

The name "Monsieur X" buzzed through the crowd virus-style, along with murmurs of astonishment. I couldn't stand it any longer.

"STOP!!!!" I shouted. "Do *not* take her picture! Please!" I begged.

Suddenly everything went dead quiet (well, as quiet as could possibly be imagined in a crowd this size), as all eyes turned to me. I glared at Minty and Ferebee. It took a few seconds, but after the anticipated lapse of memory, their eyes lit up with recognition.

"That's her!" Ferebee shouted. "That's the girl who knows where Monsieur X is! She's his . . . his . . ."

"Liaison!" Minty helped.

A *whoosh* sound and then, like a herd of buffalo on stampede, every journalist in the crowd came at us.

"Talk into this mike," said a sound guy with headphones.

"Turn this way to face the camera," said a video camera operator.

Evie and I were unceremoniously pushed in front of the models. I had to shield my eyes with the phony bags as a hundred strobes fired simultaneously. A cluster of microphones surrounded us and the questions came—each reporter outyelling the other.

"Why do you call 'im Monsieur X?"

"What is 'is real name?"

"How do you know 'im?"

"Why does 'e not speak for 'imself?"

"What's his sign, man?" This last question was from a rogue stringer for *Topanga Canyon Weekly*.

"One at a time, please!" I shouted over the din, to no effect.

"Who are you?"

"My name is Imogene and I work for Hautelaw and—"

"What's an Hautelaw?"

"It's a fashion forecasting company."

Suddenly, and with pitch-perfect timing, a voice from the crowd said, "*Alors*, y'all!" It was Mercie, bursting through the wall of reporters like a Texas tornado. Only French.

"Zees is my client and she speaks to no one but me!" Mercie announced, standing on the front line between us and the journalists. "If you have any questions for Mademoiselle Imogene, you will kindly address me! And I, in turn, will address her, who speaks directly to Monsieur X, who will give zee answer back to her, who will convey it to me, and I to you!"

"Mercie, what are you doing here?" Evie whispered in her ear.

By way of answer, she shoved the latest copy of *MMD*,

opened to page four, at us. Then she said to me, "I am your new PR agent, *chérie*!"

Too confused to process what she'd just said, let alone this whole media circus, Evie and I huddled together with Mercie for a quick scan of the *MMD* page, revealing the source of all the mayhem.

MMD: (PARIS) 9 JULY
MYSTERY COUTURIER PREMIERES AT MODEL MUTINY

The dashing designer known to le tout Paris simply as Monsieur X, to sneak peek his by all accounts marvie collection on model picket line today. This is likely to be big—big—BIG! So stay tuned, kitties, and check my column tomorrow.

—O.D.D.

Sure enough, affixed adjacent to the headline was a shot of Preppy Man. His byline, Olivier DeDompierre, appeared directly beneath his smiling face.

"Ohmigod! I knew this had something to do with him!" I fumed, nearly losing an eye on a swinging BBC mic.

"Don't worry!" Mercie whispered. "I will take care of everything. Don't say a word to these jackals. I'm your mouthpiece from here on in. I'll do all the talking."

"Where is Monsieur X?"

"Where he should be, in his atelier."

"Where is his atelier?"

"Do you think we'd tell you where the most sought-after couturier in decades is working? He needs to concentrate on his upcoming collection."

At that point, a furious Caprice had appeared out of nowhere and was threatening to punch Minty. Apparently, as I would hear later, Caprice had seen the reporters coming, and when she tried to prevent the girls from going outside, Minty had shoved her in the bathroom and barricaded the door.

My cell phone rang. I put the phone to my ear and yelled into it. "Hello?!!"

"Daaaaaahling!!!"

"Spring?!" OMG.

"You're looking better than ever, dear!"

"What?!"

"I'm watching you on television right now!"

"Television?!"

"Yes, sweetie. That screen in your living room with the funny pictures on it?"

"I don't understand."

"You're on *CNN Live*!"

"What?!"

"I said, you're on—"

"But—how? It must be four in the morning there."

"Fashion never sleeps, dear. Speaking of which, I adore what you're wearing. Kate Hepburn–chic white linen wide-legged pants are such a refreshing antidote to her distant relation and style antithesis, Audrey."

"Oh, thank you. But about today, Spring, well, I can explain. You see—"

"No need, dear. I know a brilliant publicity stunt when I see one."

"Publicity stunt? Oh . . . yes! Publicity stunt!"

"I assume you contracted that cowgirl person for the event."

"Mercie?"

"You're welcome. As I was saying, it was very shrewd on your part. Anyway, I want you to keep working with her. Whoever she is, she's hired. She's brilliant! Leaking news of Monsieur X to the press, then getting models to wear his clothing on the picket line . . ."

A long, contemplative drag from a cigarette followed.

"This media circus will do absolute wonders for retail sales! All of our retail clients have seen your coverage. The look book is a *gigantic* hit, and queries are just flooding in! Barneys is about to preorder Monsieur X's entire collection— sight unseen. And our beauty clients . . . well, suffice it to say, they're already talking *license deals*!"

Try as I might, I couldn't get a word in.

"You've got your finger on the pulse of this situation, Imogene. Leave it to you—your cutting-edge thinking is about to put us way ahead of the pack. It's all over the air-waves."

"But Spring—"

"I'm so excited I'm flying over to Paris myself! And I'm bringing Mick and Malcolm with me. Now, I want you to set up a meeting first thing with that cowgirl person—I'll be in

Paris in two shakes of a lamb's tail, dear. We've got to move into phase two of our plan."

"What plan?" I cringed, afraid to hear the answer.

"Why, presenting Monsieur X's collection to his adoring public, of course, dear."

"You mean, a show?! But what about the model strike?"

"What about the model strike? My fellow Aries, we don't follow trends—we set them!"

I moaned.

"Well, I've got an early interview scheduled with *Women's Wear Daily* and I need my beauty rest. Ta!"

Like the "Wanted" posters that once papered the Wild West, Paris became littered with "WANTED" posters of Monsieur X. Only in this case, no one (including myself) had a clue as to his identity. A black-and-white outline served in lieu of a photo.

It had become a gray, wet, cheerless Paris day. I wanted something comforting. I decided on afternoon tea. Although Salon de Thé was being held up by hideous metal scaffolding outside (no doubt to stop the roof from caving in), the shabby chic of the ornately gilded walls and pretty, painted ceilings had its particular charm. Instead of doing what Americans come to Paris cafés to do—pore over Flaubert and Camus, debate philosophy and discuss the great artistes of the day with the locals—I came to the café to get my head together.

"There she is!" someone outside the window shouted. "It's that *Hautelaw!*"

I scrunched down, pulling my out-of-season Vuitton bucket hat down low, waiting for Evie to arrive. After the media circus fiasco, Evie and Caprice zipped the clothes back to the atelier in a car Mercie had waiting, leaving everyone else to get where they were going via the land yacht.

Life as a fashion-forecasting intern in Paris has its ups and downs. Ups: Getting paid to do something you love. Downs: Being stalked by multitudes of strangers, be they tourist, reporters, or the odd fashionista left in a town where you are the only connection to the hottest couturier in the world.

A reporter banged on the window where I sat waiting for Evie to arrive. Thankfully the creepy waiter seemed delighted to shoo the reporters and tourists away.

I spotted Evie as soon as she walked through the door. When she sat down, I returned her greeting with a terse glare.

"So, you're not speaking to me?" Evie said softly.

I shook my head and waved a waiter over.

"How could I have let you talk me into this?" I cried.

Once again, there was an interruption by a new unruly crowd outside the window. And again, I scrunched down in my seat.

"See!" I said, pointing at the window without looking. "It's horrible!"

"Calm down, girlena," Evie soothed.

"I will not calm down. Satellite dishes ten deep are beaming coverage all over the world of a nonexistent designer's collection that I'm allegedly responsible for and I'm supposed to calm down? This is getting very out of control!" I shouted. "Not only that, Spring is taking orders left and right from the look book I sent her!"

"Wow! That's great!"

"That's *not* great! That's scary!"

"Okay. I know it's scary, but Mercie and I have it all figured out."

"She's lining up cosmetics deals, licensed-product deals. I'm sure there'll be dolls and movie deals to follow any minute now!"

"Girlene, listen. Do not panic. I have a plan."

"Isn't that what got me into this mess to begin with? Your plan?"

"Listen for a second. First of all, it's going to be all right. To ease your mind, I checked the house. No one is there. There haven't been any messages and the atelier hasn't been touched. Everything is like we left it. Secondly," Evie continued, "I've got a lead on our—as in Crispin Lamour's—factory. Everyone in Paris has stopped production, and with no collections to cut, they're losing money like crazy. I've told them we might come in with some orders, and they've agreed to work with us."

"How? What about seamstresses? Pattern makers? Piece goods buyers?" I continued shifting in my chair, ducking every time someone walked by the window.

"With the shows on hold, the sewers will be on hiatus. But they'd rather be working. So, after a little wrangling, they agreed to work for us."

"And how are we supposed to pay for all this, exactly? Did you ever consider that? Who's going to buy the fabric? And what *about* the seamstresses, and production costs? Who's paying for all that?"

"You are!"

"I?"

"Yes, you, my little BFF. You're flush with all that *Imogenius* cash."

But little did Evie know, I had begun sending a few *Imogenius* refunds back home, and my once flush bank account was dwindling.

date: JULY 10

With *Imogenius* on the fritz, I threw caution to the wind and pulled on a pair of no-name skinny jeans and a tank top—though I had enough sense to complete the ensemble with a highly identifiable pair of platforms. By all rights, today should have been a "pink" day. But with a clogged e-mail box due to the glut of angry *Imogenius* users (customer service was never my forte), escapist visions of the most adorable thigh-skimming, pink petal-pleated dress that I'd seen in Colette's window was all I was capable of thinking about.

chapter nine

Have Mercie!

Random quote: No great genius has ever existed without some touch of madness. —Aristotle

✳   ✳   ✳

M ercie de la Chatelaine was a blur of motion as she buzzed into her office suite at the Hotel Castille, simultaneously chattering away on two cell phones. Her landline was lit up like the Vegas strip. Her de rigueur hat, graced with a whimsical little black-and-white-striped twist, skimmed her head tightly. The twist bounced from side to side whenever she moved her head, giving her a loony, cartooney vibe.

"That's complete rubbish!" the petite powerhouse exclaimed. "They're just friends! Hold on." Click. "I'll have to get back to you on that!" She switched phones. "No, she's not having a baby! *Absolument pas!*" Click. "What?! No, he's not having a baby either!"

She held up an index finger, indicating she'd be with us shortly. Swathed in freebie Andrew Gn (I'll explain the freebie part shortly), I sashayed into the seat opposite her desk. Evie sat next to me.

Apparently it was not at all unusual to have an office in a hotel room. (I told you French girls were backward!) Quotes from great fashion legends, like Coco Chanel and Diana  Vreeland, covered the walls. Behind Mercie's desk was a picture of her posed with Mickey Mouse at Euro Disney. She was resplendent in the requisite (if you're a fan) Mickey Mouse ears cap. The shelves were filled with a collection of Disney statuettes, including a rare Tinkerbell figurine. But what caught my eye was a framed pair of jeans, which hung directly over her desk.

When she'd finished her last call, she tossed both her cell phones in her desk drawer (still ringing) and said, "Imogene! Evie!"

We kissed, kissed, kissed.

"I'm sorry you had to wait. These reporters are nefarious, you know? Especially O.D.D. Did you see his column today?"

"No," Evie and I answered in unison.

Mercie reached for the paper and passed it to me. In it were mostly quotes:

> "Today a major new designer rocked the world of fashion, without ever existing!"
>
> —Swoozie, famous gossip columnist

"I want every single thing!"

—Tinsley Vogelzang, Famous A.s.s.-ette

"Why didn't I think of that?"

—John Galliano, designer

"Rich! Rich! Rich! With Mr. X, it's all about rich. And gorgeous! I saw dollar signs walking the picket line today. Which is the point. After all, who wants to look poor?"

—Miranda Von Chantecleer, rich, rich, rich A.S.S.-ette

"It was smashing! And where did he find those models? Wow!"

—Rubirosa Mountziff, Famous A.S.S. Escort

I stood up and walked to the oversize window, looking down on the *rue* below.

"I *j'adore* your office. How fun having it in a hotel."

"It's actually my boss's apartment. The best thing about it is that it's next door to Chanel. And with Chanel comes *La Lagerfeld*! To work for him is my dream. How can I express it with mere words . . . I idolize him. I worship him. There are no words!" she said with a smile that made her porcelain blue eyes twinkle. Devotion was an understatement.

"And those jeans are amazing!" Evie said, staring at the framed jeans.

"Thank you," Mercie said proudly, curling her lips like the cat that ate the canary. "Lagerfeld is a visionary with

129

rock star power. See, he signed them — *là!*" She pointed to the inscription across the bum and legs of the jeans.

"How did you get them?"

"Oh, I have a secret. But I will tell you. My old concierge Adolfo is like zis," she said, crossing her fingers, "with the concierge at the Ritz . . . and, well, there is a side entrance on the Rue Cambon, which is *là!*" She pointed at the window. "And through it, there is a secret passageway, which leads straight to Chanel. One night, when no one was looking, Adolfo and the Ritz concierge took me there. . . ."

Okay, so her little stalking episode at the party the other night wasn't just an isolated event.

"For just a peek," she continued. "So there I was, breathing the same air that Monsieur L. breathes. Oooh, I was just swept away. Then suddenly, out of nowhere popped Monsieur. Naturally, I was frozen solid. Like zis." She demonstrated. "I could not move and I could not speak. He was with his butler — he is never alone — and they were leaving, and before I could say a word, he asked me if I wanted an autograph, but I didn't have any paper. So, voilà, like zat, he took the pen from his butler's hand and he signed them! *Incroyable!* No?"

"That *is* incredible!"

"*Oui,*" she said proudly. "So, we come to the point. Please tell Spring I am so happy to be working for her and Monsieur, and I will do the best possible job of any PR firm in all of Paris. I am just going over the press release one last time. How does zis sound? 'Spring Sommer, on

130

behalf of Monsieur X, has retained the services of Mercie de Chatelaine of the PR firm Raison d'Etre, to assist in launching Monsieur X's debut collection. . . . '"

In the mere few days since Spring had signed Mercie on, she'd been doing a phenomenal job. But like a good little PR hound, she sensed our hesitation.

"I understand, *mes amis*." Mercie gently guided us to a nearby dining table and chairs, piled high with printed material. "You do not wish to reveal the identity of your precious Monsieur X so easily. After all, he is *your* discovery. But do not worry. I am 'ere to 'elp you." She put a consoling hand on my shoulder. "Just think of me as your ally. *Bon*. So, the question remains, when can I meet him? I have a show to plan, after all. And as you know, Spring will be arriving in Paris in two more days."

Mercie was clearly one of those people who plowed through everything toward a single, fixed goal, despite any obstacles that might get thrown in her way. Even though I had just told her that Monsieur X didn't want anyone to know who he was, she was going to keep pushing until she met him. I also realized that what Evie and I needed most right then was precisely what Mercie had going for her.

I looked at Evie, who winked and decided right then and there to make her our partner in crime. So we spilled the beans about the atelier and Caprice, the phony name, everything. The only thing I didn't mention was the black Citroën that had been following me around the city ever since our media outing. In fact, I hadn't mentioned it to anyone.

Though it was probably just fashion groupies or reporters; or my overwrought imagination.

"*Magnifique!*" Mercie clapped her hands together joyously.

Finally, the topic of where to hold the inevitable fashion show came up.

"But where will you present it?" I asked.

"Why not at HLP?" Evie said enthusiastically.

"Help? What is help?"

"Hautelaw Paris. They have an office on a houseboat on the Seine," Evie explained.

"A houseboat? That is perfect!"

"We'll do a teensy guest list and say it is strictly for Monsieur's closest family and friends. That alone will drive half of Paris wild."

She snapped her BlackBerry up off her desk and began furiously punching buttons. "Monsieur X is about to make Paris go *in-sane!*"

"Wait a minute!" I shouted. "Aren't you forgetting just one tiny thing?! Like, who is Monsieur X? I mean, excuse me, but we still don't know who designed these clothes!"

Evie and Mercie stopped and stared at me. After a long and potentially embarrassing pause, Mercie flung her arms in the air and huffed.

"A minor detail! Besides, that is for you to investigate!"

"Me?!"

"But of course you! That, and shoot the show. Evie tells

me that you are an expert photographer. And judging by your video diary," she said as she thumbed through it on her BlackBerry, "I see she is correct. We'll link the show to your video diary. And from there, to the world!"

"Don't I get a say in this?" I asked nervously.

"First you have to find this Monsieur X," Mercie said resolutely, "and if you cannot find Monsieur X, I suggest you find a stand-in."

"Why me?"

"Evie has dresses to make. I have a fashion show to produce. And you? You have a designer to find!"

"But what if he's dead?"

"Impossible! Anyone that talented has got to be immortal!"

MMD: (PARIS) 13 JULY
EMERALD GREEN IS THE COLOR DU JOUR

Hey there, kitties,

O.D.D. here with the Monsieur X daily update. Seems there's a catfight brewing amongst our cité's rival hostesses to have a new couturier in their maisons. Rumor has it, though, that the shy designer has been sending his emissary, Imogene, in his stead. Competition is fierce, creating rifts all over Paris as they vie for an invitation to his first collection. Invites are rumored to be going out within days. Every A-list super-socialite worth her château is hoping to be there.

Pressure is mounting at the model union to end the strike *toute de suite*.

Stay tuned, kitties. Meow!

chapter ten

Merry Kisses and Happy New Swag

date: JULY 13

affirmation: I AM OPEN TO RECEIVE

* * *

Holy chic! It was nine a.m. The last thing I wanted was to be late to the office the day of Spring's arrival.

With Imogenius relinquished to a thing of the past, I naturally lapsed into my default alter ego: the Ingénue. I laced a couple of Ladurée ribbons around my wrists and tossed on my boudoir lace slip with ribbon trimming (Dolce & Gabbana spring '06) and a pair of cargo capris.

Moving on to shoes, I surveyed the selection. A random thought crossed my mind: Do I live to shop? Or shop to live?

When the doorbell rang, a less than cheerful Leslie shouted

for me to please answer it. I clambered downstairs, pink satin ballet slippers in hand, navigating the narrow canyons of boxes and shopping bags that had lined the staircase.

Ever since the picket-line debacle, this had become my morning routine. The doorbell began buzzing around eight a.m., followed by nonstop phone ringing until some time around midnight. Evie and I had been on every blog, newspaper, and gossip website on the planet. So naturally, every journalist, retailer, fabric maker, button maker, hand embroiderer, and fashion freak sent their compliments, in the form of gifts, directly to our front door, in the hopes of getting a teensy audience with the elusive Monsieur X. Magazine editors were fighting over who would get to photograph (or shall we say, faux-tograph) which gown first. Publicity firms on behalf of their clients (and themselves), socialites—who would have otherwise been out of town—all had hopes of scoring a meeting with Monsieur X. And Hollywood stylists were queuing up to have Monsieur X's designs on the backs of their red-carpet clients. I mean, their very reputations were at stake. Seriously, what would someone like Lindsay Lohan say when her stylist was unable to come up with the latest and greatest? Most likely something to the effect of, "You're fired!"

I quickly admonished myself, while involuntarily gobbling down a pastel-colored macaroon from one of dozens of pale green and gold Ladurée boxes. Of course I had to open every box! There was a huge assortment, and they were arranged totally fashion forecast-ey: by color story! One box was all pinks with neutrals, another, neutrals with an accent of black. The black ones were licorice flavored—not my favorite, but dramatic nonetheless!

The doorbell rang again. I replaced the Ladurée box lids and lined them up on the marble console table in the foyer. I heard Leslie trotting toward the front door.  This would probably be a good time to mention the missing bags from the Pacojet box as, no doubt, you're probably wondering if Leslie had noticed anything. All I can say is that, aside from being grumpier than usual, due to the uninterrupted invasion of our privacy, he didn't seem to have noticed a thing. In fact, Evie and I were almost certain he'd forgotten about the Pacojet altogether.

I collected my stuff, Toy included, wiggled into my shoes, and opened the front door, nearly colliding with yet another deliveryman, before flying down the spiral stairs—not knowing I was headed straight into a firestorm.

As I hit the street, a gang of ravenous photographers and frenzied fashionistas trying to outshout each other mobbed me.

"It's her!"

"That's the girl!"

"IMOGENE! Over here!"

I wedged my way through the horde, repeating the phrase "No comment" through a fixed smile, just like a seasoned media veteran.

"Imogene! Darling! Over here, *chérie*!" A mink-laden *mondaine* dripping in canary diamonds accosted me. "Have you received my little gift? I had my chauffeur drop it off last night."

But just then, before I could respond a hand extended from the crowd, holding a large bouquet of pink peonies wrapped in tissue paper and ribbons. And instead of finding a microphone stuck in my face, I found Dax's lips.

In a flash, he kissed me. Huge. French kiss. There's something about a first kiss. Like the weather, it can be totally unexpected and very hard to predict. My heart did exactly what it's supposed to do. It stopped. And I felt the sudden arrival of a deep Dior #003 Catwalk Pink blush.

Dax grabbed my hand and I grabbed Toy, and we took off down the street to his parked motorcycle—a blood-red BMW Roadster. (Paris tip No. 22: Always travel via chauffeured motorcycle.) Just before we climbed aboard, he smiled and kissed me again. This time he kissed me more deeply than before.

I was on the verge of sorting out my feelings when something even stranger happened—like one of those really weird coincidences that only take place in the movies. Seriously. Because when Dax turned the key, the clutch of reporters that had followed us parted, and I spotted the black Citroën again.

As we pulled away from the curb, the sedan pulled away too. In a flash, we were darting through city traffic.

I turned around as we crossed the Pont de la Concorde. The sedan was still there.

"We're being followed," I shouted.

Dax glanced in his rearview and smiled.

"Of course we are being followed. You are the most popular girl in Paris."

"If they were paparazzi, wouldn't they pull up next to us and shoot pictures?"

After a brief pause, Dax said, "Let's find out!"

He veered into the right lane and slowed down just enough so the Citroën could easily pull up. I caught a glimpse of the driver—OMG, it was Leslie's friend Jimmy, the guy from the warehouse! My heart pounded. My mind raced back to the warehouse. The box Leslie picked up. The bags! They were counterfeiters! And Leslie was the *ringleader*! I mean, with hair like that he was capable of anything. Then a new thought came to me: OMG! I'd been alone in the apartment with him all morning!

"What do you think they want?" Dax asked as he zipped back into traffic.

"I have no idea," I replied innocently. I absolutely *did not* want Dax to get involved in this. Whatever *this* was. Wait a minute, who was I kidding? There were no counterfeiters, and Leslie was not a criminal mastermind. I was just stressed out; that was it. Get a grip, Imogene! If Leslie knew about the bags, he could have done something about it anytime he wanted. I mean, he does *live there*. Besides, Aunt Tamara would never hire a criminal. Well, not a common one, anyway. She's more the international jewel-thief-slash-man-of-mystery type.

The black Citroën was still following us. I snapped my head forward to glance at Dax's reflection in his mirror. There was a furtive gleam in his eyes, and his muscles were tensed. The next thing I knew, Dax was heading, full throttle, straight for the stalls of the Bastille market.

"Dax, please be careful!" I moaned. Thank goodness for Paris's unspoken driving etiquette: Thou shalt not knock someone off a motorcycle or scooter because it may be your sister, your boss, or your *pâtissière*.

We shot forward like a rocket. He yanked the motorcycle to the left, whipping us back around the Place de la Concorde, then making a hard right onto the Champs-Elysées.

"The houseboat is the other way!" I shouted. Dax weaved the motorcycle in and out of heavy city traffic, but the Citroën persisted, staying exactly two cars behind. Dax jerked the handlebars to the right, and we escaped by zooming up Avenue de Matignon.

Mick, Malcolm, and I waited quietly as Spring placed a red-lacquer cigarette holder between her lips, clicked a vintage Cartier lighter, and inhaled deeply. She had on a dark green cotton turban—a perfect match to her equally dark green and very large sunglasses, vintage bathing gown, and platforms, clearly channeling silver-screen legend Paulette Goddard to perfection. The forties were making a comeback, and clearly she intended to show her clients she'd picked up on that trend first.

She leaned forward and opened a mini cosmetics refrigerator beneath her Louis XIV desk. Then she dipped an SUV-size, Burmese diamond–adorned finger into a tub of C.O. Bigelow Rose Salve lip gloss, smeared the shimmering gloss over her famously pouty lips, and spun around to face us.

"Chez d'Hautelaw is shaping up to look like quite a mini-Versailles!" she drawled happily, releasing a prodigious plume of secondhand smoke into the room.

I imagine it was her special way of christening the new office.

"Hugs!" she squealed spontaneously, and proceeded to embrace me and the boys like a mother hen come home to roost.

No one moved. Except for Spring's two overfed pugs, who must have picked up a voice cue Spring usually reserves for them and came trotting over. (A woman of the world, Spring spoke several languages, including Dog.) Spring's dogs accompanied her everywhere, and as a result of her chimney-like behavior, their once cute little *woofs* were now bellowing *bow-wows*, poor things. You'd think their mood collars, being in a perpetual state of black, would at least give her a hint.

Mick and Malcolm squirmed in silent desperation. Not that they weren't wild about Spring or anything. But as a general rule, any female love effusion, especially the overt kind and even more especially from Spring, made them want to hurl. Besides, Mick couldn't stand the idea of having his clothes anything less than perfectly pressed. He was in one of his trademark snazzy suits—black with purple pinstripes and purple shirt. A Savile Row meets sixties rocker Brian Jones thing. Malcolm was wearing his usual Village People ensemble—biker boots, black leather pants (despite the fact that it was eighty degrees outside), and black T-shirt with STUD MUFFIN emblazoned across the front in Day-Glo blue.

"Imooogeeeeene dear! Let me look at you," Spring

drawled, slipping off her retro specs. "You're looking positively fabu, dear! Paris certainly agrees with you, doesn't it? And I can't believe how much you've accomplished in so little time."

The houseboat was rapidly nearing completion, but things were still in a state of semi-upheaval. After weeks of Dax's restoration, the "bones," meaning floors, ceilings, and walls, were done, and the decoration process was in full swing. The color scheme was gold, white, and crystal in the main room; robin's egg blue, lilac, and dove gray in the others. Boiserie carved wood panels—embellished with images of the arts and sciences, music, and (you guessed it) fashion, served as the doors.

"Oy! You could plotz from the gilt," Malcolm murmured.

Paula Zee, an old model friend of Spring's turned decorator, had been specifically instructed to "outgilt" Versailles—a task, I must say, that she took deeply to heart.

While the houseboat was groaning with gilt, I was experiencing a *gilt* trip of an entirely different nature. I mean, just thinking of what would happen to me if this whole house of cards came crashing down. And right now, I didn't see how it wouldn't.

Mick glanced around the room and smiled. "You may very well have raised the gold standard."

"Yes, but something's missing . . . a theme, perhaps. What do *you* think, Mick dahling?"

"How about a heroic theme?" said Malcolm. "You know, pictorial tiles with cypress trees and statues of Adonis and—"

"The Adonis thing is over," Spring declared. "Even Versace has moved on."

"Look, why don't we all think about it," said Mick.

"Yes, let's!" said Spring. "But we do need to decide soon. After all, it has to be built in time for the show. And speaking of building . . . " Spring snuffed out her cigarette and turned to me. "Where's Dax?"

Dax was beginning to creep into my thoughts at odd times during the day. I mean, even before today's surprising *le kiss*. I'd think about his sweet smile. Or how cute he looked when he was working and not aware that I was watching him. For some reason, every time I thought of him I broke out in a volcanic eruption of giggles. Though maybe I was still shaken from the motorcycle ride over here.

"Dahling, are you all right?" The three of them were staring at me with what can only be described as a mixture of concern and alarm—except for Mick, who looked as if he were about to burst out laughing.

"Me? I'm fine!" I stammered a little too emphatically. "Why do you ask?"

"You were giggling uncontrollably, sweetie. Have you been getting enough sleep?" asked Spring.

"Sleep? Yes, lots of sleep."

"Yes, well." Spring cleared her throat. "I was asking about Dax. You remember him? Tall, blond, French . . ."

"Really?" Malcolm perked up.

"I must congratulate him on his work so far!" Spring said, plucking another cigarette from her antique enamel-and-gold cigarette case. After taking a long sip of red wine—

through a straw, so as not to stain her veneers—she said, "Now, to the point of this meeting. Thanks to Imogene, our new business venture is coming together. You know, it's just as my astrologer said, the Sun is trining my Jupiter in my house of work. The perfect backdrop for a major business alliance! After all, it's high time Hautelaw branched out. Licensing is where it's at, dears. You know, everyone's into making all sorts of deals with designers these days. And I just *love* sponsoring young new designers. The younger the better! He is young, isn't he, dear?" she said nervously.

I shifted nervously in my chair. By now my stomach was churning. I have never been a good liar.

"Which reminds me, dear. I'd like him to sign our letter of agreement as soon as possible." Spring peered at me over her shades and smiled. "When *do* we get to meet our new genius behind the seams?"

"I'm arranging it as we speak, Spring." I gulped.

Somehow I must have given Spring the impression that she'd be meeting Monsieur X. And that he'd be signing an exclusive contract with her to represent him on every level. She was beyond thrilled that she would be the only other soul alive to find out his true identity.

"He'll have to start thinking accessories. He has to be commercially viable—you know, handbags, shoes. Like that. Speaking of which, Bergdorf's, Bloomie's, and Barneys are making sounds about a trunk show, and they've already presold out of everything in Monsieur X's debut collection— sight unseen! Nordstrom and Jeffrey are breaking down the door to have him, and I can't tell you how many other retailers are lining up. And don't think for a moment that I'm ungrateful, Imogene. You are up for a big, big, big bonus for this one!"

I was beyond queasy as Spring continued rattling off a laundry list of business ventures, pending license agreements, and even potential reality TV show pitch ideas; my heart had begun beating faster than a hummingbird's. Shortness of breath was imminent, as was *fat-ee-gay*, which would have been stress if we were in the U.S., because no one in Paris has stress. They have *fatigue*.

"Well then, as our plans are all under control, thanks to our Imogene, the only thing left to arrange is the show," Spring said. "Mercie and I have a meeting scheduled for this afternoon. Mick, Malcolm, I'll want you in on that meeting. Imogene, you'll be arranging the meeting with Monsieur X. Be sure to call me on my cell as soon as it's set, dear. I'll be waiting."

At that moment, I had to ask myself, do I really have what it takes to succeed as a fashion forecaster?

It was time to find out the answer for sure.

To: Imogene
Fr: Cissy
Re: HELP!
Dear Imogene,
As you now know, there is the worst kind of bug in *Imogenius*. Please send cash home quick!
The angry mob on my front lawn is demanding a swift refund!

chapter eleven

Planes, Trains, and Golf Carts, (and Helicopters Too!)

MMD: (PARIS) 16 JULY

Hello, kitties,

Last year's cat prints are in for a reprisal. The claws are flying in all directions while our young fashion forecaster hunts for the biggest cat of all: Monsieur X. Don't tell a soul, but I hear she's on the night train to Nice in for a rendezvous with the next hottest thing. —O.D.D.

ast night, after several hours of attempting to contact Aunt Tamara (her cell phone voice mail implied that she was in midair between Cape Hatteras and Narita

Airport), she finally replied. Once she recovered from the shock of the secret room in her building, she, of course, deferred to Georges — the man who knows everything. She told me that Georges was on his yearly sabbatical to Grand-Hotel du Cap-Ferrat, a spa in the south on the Côte d'Azur.

I left a brief note for Leslie (I still couldn't bring myself to believe he was mixed up in any criminal activity), packed a few things, and without further adieu, Caprice and I headed for Gare du Nord station.

In a last-ditch effort at French chic, I paid homage to Brigitte Bardot and ventured forth all tousled hair, pouty lips, and a pink gingham, with a puff of E Moi parfum for ultimate effect — *Imogenius* or no *Imogenius*.

Thinking of my *Imogenius* SoftWear gave me a petite panic attack. Let's just say that after a few hundred threatening e-mails, I thought it best, in order to avoid any potential lawsuits, to cut my losses and dole out the final refunds to every last subscriber. Between that and the cash I'd given Evie for the collection, roughly speaking, that left me with just about enough cash for two round-trip night train tickets to the Côte d'Azur.

"Listen to this." Caprice sighed, perusing the hotel's spa brochure, as the train hurtled forward. "'Feel your melancholy slip away as you indulge in the world of thalassotherapy, thermalism, aromatherapy, stone therapy, reflexology, shiatsu, exfoliation, and —'"

"As wonderful as that sounds, Caprice, we have to find Georges first."

Just as I said that, I happened to glance at the rear of the train car and spotted Leslie! He was sitting in the last booth. His back was to me, but I'd recognize that wind-tunnel coif anywhere. Further confirmation came from the small, rodent-like man facing me. Jimmy from the warehouse. Jimmy from the black Citroën! He was busy pretending not to look in my direction. I slid down in my seat and started freaking.

"Ohmigod!" I whispered. "O.D.D.'s column must have tipped Leslie off—look!"

"Housekeeper Leslie? The one with the hair? Where?" she asked.

"No! No! Don't look! Just pretend we're having a normal, pleasant conversation. Smile a lot." I took several deep breaths.

"Maybe he's going on vacation or something. People do that, you know," Caprice said calmly.

"Except that the other guy—the one facing us?"

"Yeah?"

"That's his partner in crime, Jimmy."

"Maybe they're just traveling together. As in *ménage à deux*."

"They're not! Leslie's totally straight."

"One never knows these days."

"Well, *I* know. Besides, Jimmy's the one who gave Leslie the Pacojet box in the first place!"

"And what was in the box?"

"Ladies' bags."

"I rest my case," she said smugly. "So? You put the bags back in the box, right?"

I looked at Caprice and suddenly had that sinking

sensation. You know, the one where you feel like you're stuck in quicksand and keep sinking deeper and deeper and you can't move or breathe and your stomach starts doing flip-flops?

"Not exactly," I squeaked. "I mean, we still need them for the show. Evie and I replaced them with her stuffed animals until we can put the bags back."

Caprice rolled her eyes. "Okay, so there's still no reason to think he knows anything. As long as the box is still there."

"Well . . ."

Caprice exhaled. "Don't tell me."

"When I was packing, I went to get my overnight bag out of the closet and I noticed it was gone."

Caprice's brows shot up. "Are you kidding me? Was Leslie there?"

"No! And that's the weird thing. I mean, he said he was going away for a few days and wouldn't be back until late next week. That was *yesterday*!"

"Ohmigod! He's after us!" Caprice slid down and peered around the corner of her seat. "What do we do now?"

I spotted a waiter pushing a dinner trolley down the aisle.

"Get down!" I whispered.

As the trolley rolled past, toward Leslie and company, I pulled her through the doorway and into the next car. I figured we could quietly zip through the other eight or so cars to our sleeper, then bolt the door behind us. As we raced into the club car, we were ambushed by a gaggle of couture-clad

A-list super socialites, who blocked the aisle like the offensive line of the New York Giants—only scarier.

Their apparent leader, upon spotting me shouted, "*Mademoiselle, mademoiselle!* But, this is just the *coïncidence incroyable, n'est-ce pas*?"

Though she looked familiar, I couldn't quite place her.

"Remember me?" she said, catching up with us.

"*Non.* I mean, no."

"We were conversing outside your house. I'm sure you remember my chauffeur. You did receive my little prezzie, I hope."

"Oh, yes. Thank you. Such a thoughtful gift." Not that I remembered which one of the gazillion boxes was her gift.

"You're quite welcome." She smiled with a sigh of relief. "Perhaps you would join us in the dining car. Our little group is *very interested* in making your acquaintance." She smiled charitably at Caprice. "And your friend, of course."

"Oh, I'm sorry, we really don't have time—"

"Wait a minute," growled Caprice. "How did you know she was on this train?"

The couture sisterhood tittered in unison—no doubt they'd had their chauffeurs follow us to the train. I glanced over my shoulder and caught sight of Leslie and Jimmy madly struggling to get past the food trolley.

"Listen, we really have to be going." I began to move, but Madame's pals closed ranks, forming an impenetrable wall of aristocratic bulk.

"Hey!" Caprice snapped. "Move it or lose it, *chiquita*!"

"But *mademoiselle* . . . about Monsieur X. Can we count on an invitation?"

"Please, *mademoiselle*, we'll do anything," her friend pleaded.

I decided to punt. "You know what?" I said, leaning forward confidentially. "I really shouldn't say anything but, well, you seem so nice and everything. So I'm going to let you in on a secret."

"Yeeeeesss?" Her eyes widened. "Yeeeeesss?"

"Well, you see those two men in the car behind us?"

"The ones fighting with the waiter?" she asked doubtfully.

When I looked again, Jimmy and the waiter were piled on the floor wrestlemania-style, while Leslie attempted to climb over them—without much success.

"Exactly. Well, the big one . . ."

"With the blowout?"

"Yes." I nodded. "That's *Monsieur X*!"

She looked at me in disbelief. Then horror.

"He *always* travels in disguise," I confided.

"Who is that small rodentlike person on the floor?"

"That's his bodyguard."

Caprice and I barely escaped being trampled to death as the couture sisterhood stormed the next car. In a way, I felt sorry for Leslie. I mean, not even a crook should have to endure what he was about to go through.

"Listen," Caprice said, sprinting up the aisle, "if your housekeeper and that society gasbag followed us on the train there's no telling who else is on board."

Truer words were never spoken. We had no sooner

made it to the next car than two official-looking men in dark suits approached us. The first one, short with straight black hair, olive skin, and a unibrow, stared at a picture in his hand, then flashed a badge.

"I am Chief Inspector Fitz of the Sûreté and this is Inspector Piggot."

"I'm sorry, did you say Piglet?" I asked.

"Piggot. P-I-G-G-O-T."

Inspector Piggot—smallish, balding, a little portly, with a big nose and a tidy little mustache—was one of those people whose face was set into a permanent expression of mild alarm. Like he spent every waking moment in preparation of being startled, which, I imagine, was partly due to a set of restless beady eyes. Piggot glanced at us, nodded, and went back to scanning the car for things that might shock him.

"Ohmigod!" I heaved. "I'm so glad you found us! We're being chased by criminals!"

Needless to say, this was exactly the kind of moment Piggot lived for.

"Are you all right?" Caprice stared back at him, which seemed to startle him even more.

"He is fine," Fitz snapped, his double chin jiggling. Then a patient smile broke out. "You are Mademoiselle Imogene, *non*?" He held up a not-so-flattering laminated news photo taken outside the picket line. The one where I'm standing next to Evie with a deer-in-the-headlights look on my face.

"Is that from *Le Monde*? You know, I have better ones. . . ."

"Please! Mademoiselle." Fitz took a deep breath. "We

have—that is, the Sûreté has—information that you are in possession of a number of counterfeit bags."

"Yes, well, I can explain that."

Fitz held up his hand. "There is no need to explain. We are aware of how you came into possession of, how you say . . ."

"Contraband?" I said.

"Unlawful items. However, under the circumstances we, that is, the Sûreté, are willing to . . . "

"Look the other way?"

"If you will tell us the whereabouts of the bags, I would be most grateful."

"I'm sorry," Caprice interrupted, "you must not have heard correctly. Those bags? The ones you're so anxious to get your hands on? Well, the *really bad guys* who made them are chasing us as we speak!"

"What did you say?" Fitz said in disbelief.

As if on cue, Piglet's eyes nearly popped out of his head. He grabbed Fitz by the shoulder and pointed at the window of the next car. Everyone turned at once. There, barreling down the aisle, was a very angry Leslie (completely disheveled), followed by Jimmy, now sporting a black eye, with an equally enraged couture sisterhood at their heels.

"OHMIGOD!!" I jumped behind Fitz. "That's them! The counterfeiters! The ones who are after us!"

"The one in the Adidas tracksuit?"

"It's Prada!" I shouted.

Fitz looked at me, then at Leslie, then at me again.

"Well, what are you waiting for?" Caprice shoved Piglet forward. "Arrest them!"

Leslie and company were already halfway through the car at that point, which meant the only thing left to do was run, which is exactly what Caprice and I did. I chanced a look back as we plunged through the next three cars, but the inspectors were gone, and even weirder, so were Leslie and Jimmy. Which made me even more nervous than I already was. I mean, even if we did make it back to our sleeper in one piece, there was no guarantee they wouldn't figure out where we were hiding.

We plummeted through to the next car, headfirst into a major three-ring-circus dance party. There was everything from a Hindu snake charmer DJ blasting Euro hip-hop (legs folded behind head, natch!) to dancing chihuahuas (*fabulous* in pink chiffon) to midget fire-eaters (resigned to smoking Gauloises while indoors). They even had a female human cannonball in black patent-leather jumpsuit and silver-etched helmet — *très chic!*

The car was packed tighter than the day-after-Christmas sale at Bloomingdale's, and getting through to the next car in a hurry wasn't going to be easy. Caprice took the plunge; I followed.

"Who are these people?!" I hollered at Caprice, barely squeezing my way through a troupe of jugglers in purple and silver rayon jumpers. Caprice hollered something over her shoulder and then was swallowed up by the crowd. I tried to shove my way past a fat lady in a sequined, neon orange tutu and matching feathered headdress, but I was bounced back into a hugely towering man in an electric blue suit.

"I'm sorry!" I hollered politely. "It's a little crowded in here!"

"You *are* in a hurry," he boomed suavely in a thick Russian accent.

He was probably, like so many Russians in France, a descendant of some grand duchess sent packing by the Bolsheviks. Understated, but speaking volumes in refined elegance.

He leaned forward and bowed. "Zaborokov the Great, at your service."

"Hi."

"You must forgive my friends. Our bus had some mechanical trouble."

"Oh?" I said quizzically.

"Ah, permit me to explain," he said. "We are traveling to the International Circus Festival of Monte Carlo. And these"—he waved his arm magnanimously around the car—"are performers. They have been working hard and are very much in need of some recreation."

"So I see. And what do you do, Mr. . . . ?"

"It is my esteemed pleasure to perform extraordinary acts of illusion, incantation, and prestidigitation before the great heads of Europe."

"You're a magician!" I laughed. (Who doesn't *j'adore* magicians?)

He doffed his great hat and bowed again. "And clairvoyant. A trait I inherited from my great-great-grandmother—a distant cousin of Rasputin," he added privately with a wink. "Perhaps I can be of help."

"Help?" I gulped nervously as my stomach went back to doing somersaults. "What makes you think I need help?"

Caprice suddenly appeared. "There you are! Look, sweetie." She hooked my arm and glanced at Z. "We're in a hurry, remember?"

"I do not wish to sound forward, *mademoiselle*. As I was saying to your friend, I believe you are being followed—"

"Z is clairvoyant," I told her.

She yanked my arm. "Yes, well, as interesting as that is—"

" . . . by two men, a large one and a small one. I sense the large one is very upset."

Caprice stopped pulling at me and stared at him.

"That's amazing! How do you do it?"

"It is simplicity itself. I merely raise my head like this, and look over the heads of the crowd, and there they are." He glanced toward the back of the train, then back to us. "They are closing in."

"We have to go!" I shouted, shouldering the fat lady, with Caprice behind, shoving me.

"I think perhaps," said Z with a twinkle in his eye, "there is an easier way."

After a quick huddle with the nearby circus acts, and a firm push, Caprice and I dove into Z's magician's trick closet, and before you could say "presto, change-o," with some greasepaint and a few borrowed costume items, Caprice and I emerged as a plate-spinning mime act dubbed "The Mysterious Spinsters." With our pink-and-orange brocade bodysuits, black silk capes, and matching Zorro masks it was impossible to tell us from the rest of the fray. Okay, so maybe we didn't win any style points, but we did manage to pass unrecognized when Leslie and Jimmy plowed past us. As I reached for the sleeper car handle, Caprice grabbed me.

"What!?"

"Look!" she whispered, pointing through the window.

Sure enough, Brooke was leaning against the open door of a compartment, talking to the Salad Sisters inside. She was logo-ed to death (circa early Nicole Richie).

"Oh, great!" I sighed. "The Wolfe Pack is off their leash!"

"Listen," Caprice said, looking over her shoulder, "we only have a few minutes before your housekeeper catches up with us."

After what seemed like an eternity of nonstop Brooke blather (more than thirty seconds of her is an endless loop of monotony), the door of the neighboring compartment slid open and Candy appeared.

(Affirmation: I have positive, loving, supportive relationships with all the people in my life.)

She quickly stepped inside Brooke's sleeper and slid the door closed. Caprice and I tiptoed past the compartment and could just hear Brooke's muffled voice. Needless to say, the temptation to eavesdrop was irresistible.

"What did Winter say this time?" Candy sneered.

"She wants me to make that little witch an offer," Brooke said.

"What kind of offer?"

"She said she could have eight percent of all licensing deals, *and* she'll make her a partner in the business."

"She's not serious!" cried Romaine.

"Of course she's not serious. But that doesn't mean Greenwich girl won't fall for it."

"She won't if she hears it from you." Fern chuckled.

"She's not going to hear it from me, stupid. She's going to hear it from the horse's mouth. All *you* have to do is find her. Winter will take care of the rest."

"Winter can be *soooo* convincing," Candy oozed.

"Especially for that chick from the sticks," Romaine added, followed by a group snicker.

"Okay," Brooke barked, "we know she's somewhere on the train. Just spread out and call me as soon as you spot her. Do not engage, understand?"

The door flew open and Brooke caught us by surprise. We tried to move out of her way, but it was too late. The rest of the Wolfe Pack filed into the hallway and blocked the passage. We didn't dare say anything to them, so everyone just stood there and stared at one another.

"I'm all out of candy, try the next house," Brooke finally snipped. The pack broke into peals of laughter.

"Let me guess," Candy chimed in. "Somebody called for a superhero but they sent you two instead."

More laughter.

I resisted the urge to punch her in the nose and tried to squeeze past.

158

"Wait a minute." Brooke put her hand against the far wall and narrowed her eyes. "You look familiar."

I shrugged and looked at Caprice. She shrugged too, but I could see her eyes how furious she was.

"Oh, I get it," said Fern. "You're mimes."

"I *hate* mimes!" added Romaine.

I opened my mouth and patted it with my hand like I was yawning, thinking maybe they'd get the hint that we wanted to leave.

"Oh look, girls, that's mime-speak for 'we're tired,'" Brooke said. "Maybe you're tired because you're so very *boring*."

She dropped her arm and we slipped past to our compartment.

"Maybe it's not you," Candy yelled after us. "Maybe your act is just tired."

As tired as I was, I kept thinking about Georges and how even if I found him there was no guarantee that he would know who Monsieur X was. Even if he did, he might not know where he was. Either way, I had to stay optimistic. I mean, all I really had going for me at that point was hope. And that was enough.

When I finally did fall asleep, it was to the echo of howling wolves.

chapter twelve

Woe is Moi

date: JULY 17

To Do: Write a novel, buy a château, let my eyelashes grow, compliment at least one person per day, get reacquainted with inner self, and avoid traumatic experiences at all costs.

✳   ✳   ✳

The next morning found us on a chartered bus barreling down the coastal route toward the peninsula in the company of Z and the rest of the troupe (Leslie, Jimmy, the couture sisterhood, and the Wolfe Pack had been waiting in ambush by the taxi stands). Hats off to Z for the costumes and the ride.

In terms of geography, we were somewhere between Cannes and Nice. The bus wound its way over the death-defyingly narrow road to *route de plages*. We drove past the rugged hills of cypress and oleander with stunning meadows of cornflower blue and shades of pink that ravaged the senses and blanketed the whitewashed cliffs and terra-cotta buildings. Every so often I caught glimpses of the sea to one side before we descended into a stunning landscape of lavender, mimosa, grapevines, and bamboo.

The driver, following our instructions, pulled into the white-pebbled circular driveway of the Grand-Hotel du Cap-Ferrat. Tall cedars stabbed the eternal blue sky, which was matched by the deep turquoise blue sea beyond. (They don't call it the Côte d'Azur for nothing.) The aging tour bus deposited us, looking like two rejects from a comic book convention (luggage included), on the marble doorstep.

I mean, not that we weren't grateful for the ride or anything, but I was hoping to arrive at *l'hotel* a hair more under the radar. But since that clearly hadn't happened, we resorted to wearing our Zorro masks to avoid any further possibility of recognition.

We sauntered into the lobby without incident, leaving the greeting staff, mouths agape, in our wake (though I half expected someone to stop to ask us to rescue their cat out of a tree).

Sumptuously carved archways framed an open-air lobby, lovingly appointed with sun-yellow-and-white-striped sofas that sat on white Carrera marble floors.

Caprice stayed hidden behind a large palm while I braved the front desk to check us in. A thin woman in a gray suit, with heavy black-rimmed glasses and short red hair looked at me without blinking an eye—clearly she was a woman who'd seen everything.

"*Oui, mademoiselle?*"

"Hello," I replied, trying to impart as much urbanity as

I possibly could, given the circumstances. "I'm looking for a guest."

She smiled pleasantly.

"His name is Georges."

"Georges?" She paused, waiting for a last name.

I stared back blankly, suddenly realizing that I didn't know Georges's last name. I mean, how could I be so *duh*?!

"Uh, *Monsieur* Georges," I said, using my "how could you not know" inflection. "He has white hair, dresses in . . ." I was having trouble. I mean, he wasn't the most stylish of men. Nor was he a person with a specific style. In fact, he was sort of . . . blah.

The woman held up her hand. "I am sorry *mademoiselle*, we do not divulge the whereabouts of our guests. It is against our policy."

With that, she picked up the phone and went back to whatever it is hotel concierges do.

"Look." I broke down. "I really need to find him. I mean he, *really is* a friend of mine."

"So much so that you do not even know his surname."

"Yes, well . . . we're very casual."

"So it would seem," she replied, giving my outfit the once-over with a wintry smile. "Perhaps you'd like to rent a cabana for the day?"

Not a bad idea.

After a quick change of clothes and a short ride down the rocky cliffs on the hotel's adorable little funicular, we arrived at the celebrated Club Dauphin, with its supersize salt-water pool overlooking the dazzling Côte d'Azur. What could be more fabulous?

In the cabana, I'd slipped into a white strapless Celine bikini and a white eyelet baby-doll cover-up. After several revitalizing whiffs of warm salt air mixed with orange gel Bain de Soleil, I was ready. Caprice headed poolside in search of Georges. As for *moi*, I headed to the beach for my search.

The scene was beyond! Ultrachic, ultraslim, ultra-towel-turbaned women in Rosa Cha bikinis and cover-ups slunk out of their daylong cabanas, heading for their rooms to nap after a morning of seaside relaxation, while deeply tanned men in classic old-school bathing suits (no board shorts allowed) and Ray-Bans cruised the hot white sands. Unfortunately, not even a hint of Georges.

Endless baskets of crudités, grilled breads with aioli, sumptuous melons, wafer-thin Parma ham, grilled fish, and a host of other delicacies decorated a buffet table only slightly shorter than Long Island. I thought it best, however, to query the maître d' for possible Georges sightings before indulging.

"Excuse me," I chirped sweetly to the ennui-enshrouded maître d'. He ignored me. (Don't they all?) His eyes remained focused out to sea.

"Excuse me," I repeated, a tad louder.

This time he slowly turned his head in my direction. He took one look, then dropped his lids as if suddenly bored to the point of narcolepsy.

"*Oooooui?*" he drawled.

"I'm sorry, but I'm looking for someone and I wondered if you might have seen him."

"Perhaps. Everyone dines at the club."

"His name is Georges. Don't ask me his last name because I don't know it. But he has white hair and only wears black — although maybe since he's on vacation he's dressing a little more casually. I'm not sure about that. Anyway, he's short, like you. I mean, not that you're short or anything, because you're not. I mean, people your height are very common. Not that you're common as in ordinary, of course . . ."

"I have seen him." He sighed disdainfully.

"You have? That's great! Do you know what room he's in?"

"*Oooooui.*"

I waited for more information, but there wasn't any. Well, not without a couple of well-placed euros, anyway. Unfortunately, my baby doll was sans pockets, which meant sans cash. I was about to dash back to the cabana and grab some cash when he suddenly caught sight of something and froze, as did everyone else. There was that universal gasp again. I spun around in amazement, along with everyone else, at Caprice.

She moved across the pool deck with the sexy grace of a panther. Her floppy white sun hat and white, jeweled string bikini were all she wore (unless you counted her Chanel No. 5). With a dose of good health, a gorgioso bod, glowing summer skin, and the amazing backdrop of the Côte d'Azur, who needs clothing?

She sauntered up to the maître d' and stopped. A wry smile played on her lips.

"*Bonjour*," she purred, gazing down at him through long, dense lashes.

"*Bonjour, mademoiselle*," he stammered.

"I see you have met my friend."

"Your friend?" Beads of sweat appeared on his brow.

"Uh-huh." She moved closer, breathing heavily. "She's in a bit of a jam right now and I just know that someone with your obvious *capabilities* . . . you are in charge, are you not?"

"*Oui, mademoiselle*."

"Good," she said with a smile, smoothing his lapel. "Well then," she said, letting her vibe hang in the air. She raised her eyebrows.

He turned bright crimson, and for a moment I thought he was going to launch into spasms. Instead he swallowed loudly, mopped his forehead with a white cloth napkin, and adjusted his tie. Having put himself back together, he glanced around and then leaned forward confidentially.

"Monsieur Georges was just here. He ate a light lunch of yogurt and fresh berries and went to the spa." He checked his watch. "His fangotherapy begins at one o'clock."

"So he *is* here!" I whispered with a sudden rush of relief.

"He has been coming for many years—always the same time, always the same room; number 307. In the south wing."

"Thank you," Caprice cooed.

I was all for sprinting back to the spa and wrangling Georges right away, but Caprice insisted on something to eat while we had the chance. With little sleep and no breakfast I wasn't about to argue. Anyway, I was in the middle of filling my plate with all manner of goodies when I just happened to check out the Valentino'ed woman next to me. She was channeling Elizabeth Taylor circa 1966. I noticed she was reading *MMD*, specifically O.D.D.'s latest contribution to the world of faux journalism. It must have been a late edition. I casually took a step back and glanced over her shoulder.

HAUTELAW RALLIES FOR EXCLUSIVE WITH ELUSIVE

Hello, kitties!

Word has it that Hautelaw rising star Imogene and bombshell supermodel pal Caprice were seen boarding the night train for Nice yesterday. You can take it from meow, this sudden urge to travel can mean only one thing—a clandestine tête-à-tête with the fashion world's most sought-after misanthrope, Monsieur X.

With X's upcoming debut, former supermodel-turned-chief of Hautelaw, Spring Sommer, has dropped in on the City of Light to put a few last-minute touches on the show's locale: Hautelaw's superchic new Paris HQ.

Stakes are stellar as hotshot brass from the world's top retailers hop the pond for the big event, looking to ink a mega licensing deal. But doubts persist about Monsieur X's existence.

According to longtime Spring Sommer rival and reviler, Winter Tan, Monsieur X is a phantom devised by renegade forecaster Imogene and wannabe publicity dissident Mercie de la Chatelaine.

"I have no doubt Monsieur X will turn out to be Monsieur Zed," Winter Tan told yours truly. "This is merely part of an elaborate ruse to draw attention to Spring's Paris operation in order to steal my French clients."

Phantom or no, Hautelaw faces challenges of a more corporeal nature, vis à vis the ongoing model strike, which continues to plague the industry. Agents and talent are still at odds over limo colors, beauty naps, and swag gouging, with no real solutions in sight.

Either way, the growing list of who's who promises to make this would-be show the interstellar social event of the new millennium. But be warned, kitties, invites are scarce. And if last week's catfights were any indication of the type of frenzy elicited by this extraordinary couturier, next week should be an all-out fashion fracas.

Meow for now. —O.D.D.

"Ohmigod! May I see that?" I asked, snatching the *MMD* out of La Liz's hands without pride.

She glared at me and huffed, "Relaxation therapy is in the spa, *chérie*. I suggest you schedule an appointment."

167

My initial surprise was quickly replaced by a wave — make that a *tsunami* — of paranoia. I mean, what if we were spotted . . . again? I mean, all those socialites and style devoteés who evacuated Paris for the summer because of the strike. Well, they had to go somewhere, didn't they? And that somewhere was right where I was standing.

A nearby couple stood up and headed for the pool, leaving a green and white floppy hat behind. I casually yanked it over my head, pulled the sides down to avoid possible recognition, and went in search of Caprice (yet again). OMG! Caprice! I mean, I could probably slip by unnoticed, but Caprice was a known commodity!

I spotted her at the end of the buffet table, chatting with a distinguished-looking man in his early thirties. (I would have noticed how deadly handsome and incredibly sexy he was if I hadn't been completely overwhelmed with anxiety.) I sidled over as inconspicuously as possible.

"Oh, Imogene." Caprice smiled, nibbling some grapes. "This is Eduard August-Reynard, the CEO of EAR," she said, basking under the sun *and* Eduard's hotter than hot gaze.

"Hi," I murmured, pulling my hat as far down on my head as humanly possible. "Uh, listen . . ."

"What's wrong with your hat?" Caprice asked.

"Nothing . . . I mean, I don't want it to blow away in a sudden gust of wind. You know," I said, chuckling, "these Mediterranean breezes can be pretty fierce."

The two of them stared at me in silence.

"Listen, Caprice. I need to speak to you for a second."

"I'd love to, sweetie, but Eduard and I—"

"It's reeeaaally important," I said, pulling her over toward the gratin de fruits.

"What's the matter with you?!" she hissed. "Do you have any idea who that is?"

"Some really, really handsome guy. Listen—"

"He's not just *any* handsome guy. He's *theeee* handsome guy! As in the head of one of the largest media companies in the known universe!"

I shoved O.D.D.'s column at her. "Just read this!"

Her expression went from anger to alarm as she read.

"Great!" she huffed, pulling the sides of her hat down. "Give me a sec."

She walked over to Eduard, whispered something in his ear that made him do a full-body blush, and hurried back, tittering. From there we made a beeline for the exit, sacrificing our celebrity status (and my peripheral vision). Unfortunately, moving through the lunch rush proved somewhat hazardous.

I mean, when you really think about it, it was perfectly logical that we would collide with a waiter hoisting a tray full of food, and, of course, profoundly reasonable that *everyone* in the restaurant would suddenly stop what they were doing and stare at us. Then they'd immediately recognize Caprice, and then me, and put the pieces together. Right? Because, that is *exactly* what happened next.

"LOOK!!" someone shouted. "It's . . . THEM!!!"

"That's the girl I sent a Fendi shrug to and she never so

much as sent a thank-you note!" a woman yelled from somewhere in the back of the club.

Mental note: Call Laura at Smythson to reorder personalized note cards.

"Well, *I* sent her an Hermés throw and never even got as much as an e-mail!" shouted another.

The French are nothing if not sticklers for etiquette.

"Hah! I *personally* dropped off a year's worth of gift certificates for facials from L'Appartement 217, and got zip in return! Hey, that's my hat!"

The natives were clearly getting restless. Caprice looked at me suspiciously. "What are they talking about?"

"I have no idea," I fibbed, backing into a low railing that separated the restaurant from the pool, "but I think we'd better be going soon."

"I think maybe you're right," Caprice murmured back. "By the looks of them, they're out for blood. At the very least an invitation!"

"On three," I whispered. "One, two . . . THREE!"

We vaulted over the railing and hit the pool deck running.

"Follow that chic!" someone hollered.

I hurtled over a chaise longue, grabbing a Leonard de Paris tunic off the back and handed it to Caprice.

"Put this on!" I shouted.

A waiter leaped out in front of us, shouting and waving his hands. Caprice jammed her arm through a tunic sleeve and straight-armed him like a fullback, sending him sprawling into the pool.

"The funicular!" she hollered.

We sprinted toward the far end of the pool, behind us the

slap, slap, slap of beach sandals closing in fast. I made up a funicular mantra, praying it would be waiting for us when we got there. It was — and with a bonus! Standing there, casually holding the door open, was media tycoon Eduard, and (if she had any say in it) Caprice's newest conquest.

"Hurry!" he shouted.

The door slammed behind us as a swarm of indignant jet-setters piled up outside, jeering and pounding on the cage. Eduard smiled faintly and thrust the controls forward, and up we went, leaving the Club Dauphin and its riot of angry aristocrats in our wake.

"I have a golf cart waiting up top," he said casually.

Caprice and I wheezed our thank-yous, then collapsed on the seat, out of breath.

Sure enough, a golf cart, complete with gentleman's gentleman, was waiting for us at the top. Eduard reached down and punched a large red button on the control panel, shutting down the funicular. "Where to?" he said, smiling.

"The spa, please," I replied, and off we sped.

We traversed the grounds at record (golf cart) speed. I was beginning to breathe a little easier as we turned up the main drive, rolling beneath the great broad palms that encircled the front lawn. Unfortunately, it was not to last.

"This is your stop, but I'm afraid you won't have much time," Eduard said as we pulled up to the hotel.

We spun around and could just make out, in the distance, throngs of beachy socialites clambering over the top of the rocky cliffs, sprinting toward the hotel.

"I'll meet you out back in the gardens," Eduard said.

Caprice leaned forward and gently touched his lower lip. "We'll be there."

She grabbed my hand and we headed back inside toward the spa. After twenty-four hours of being stalked, hounded, scorned, and in general, unappreciated, I was ready to sign up for some serious therapy at the spa. And if it weren't for the fact that we were currently being chased by an angry mob, I would have done exactly that. Sadly, our visit was limited to running down hallways and bursting into various private rooms where people, and the occasional pampered pet, were being oiled, exfoliated, wrapped, mud-packed, and massaged to within an inch of their lives.

Georges was eventually located in the sauna after an undaunted Caprice strutted through the men's shower, demanding to know where he was. The news about Monsieur X, however, was not what I had hoped for. Not even close.

After fifteen minutes of backstory, explaining how we found him, Georges, who was sitting down on a bench near the indoor pool, said, "I am afraid, *mademoiselle*, that I cannot help you. I have no information."

Somehow I hadn't been expecting Georges to say that, but then I guess I hadn't really been paying attention to the facts — just my feelings. And right then, I felt tears of desperation beginning to well up.

"But you must have known about the atelier," I pleaded. "I mean, all those years in that building? How could you *not* have known?"

Georges shrugged his shoulders and sighed. "I am merely

a concierge. I bring up the mail, I sweep the floor. . . ." He turned his hands over and studied them, as if wishing they could have done more for him in this life. He sighed and placed them gently on his knees.

"This Monsieur X," he said. "Perhaps he is dead, *non*?"

"No. No, he's not dead, Georges. He's alive. I know it . . . I can feel it!"

"But the atelier, as you say, it was not touched for many years. If Monsieur X is alive, why would he have abandoned it?"

"I don't know. Maybe he had to walk away from it for some reason. Maybe he was *too good*. You know? I mean, you should see his work, Georges. It's amazing. Incredible. There's never been anyone like him!"

Georges took a while to ponder what I had said. Finally he said, "I wish I could help you, but . . ."

"But Georges," the words were beginning to stick in my throat, "if we don't help him, this fashion mystery might never be solved. And this incredible talent, whoever he is, will go or has already gone to his grave undiscovered. Nameless. It would be a tragedy if only a trace of him exists. It's the saddest thing. You have to see that, Georges," I cried, "don't you see that?"

Now I was sobbing. For the first time in my life I felt defeated. I'd hit the end of the road. There was nothing left to do but go back to Paris and face everyone *without* Monsieur X. What would happen? How was I going to explain this to Spring, and Evie, and Mercie, and everybody else who was counting on me to find him?

"I don't suppose," I hiccuped, "that you could stand in for him? I mean, no one will ever be the wiser."

Georges just looked at me sympathetically and handed me a towel to wipe my eyes. Then he looked away in contemplative silence. A sad smile broke out on his face. A glimmer of hope twinkled inside of me. Then he shook his head and quietly said, *"Non."*

"I didn't think so," I sniffled.

chapter thirteen

X Marks the Spot

date: JULY 19

mood: X-TREMELY X-HAUSTED

Random message to the universe:
To whom it may concern,
Whoever it is sticking pins in me, please stop it immediately!

✳   ✳   ✳

Life would have been so much easier had I been kidnapped by aborigines or eaten by giant sea turtles rather than returning to Paris *sans* Monsieur X. I had to admit, though, that we were all lucky to be *anywhere* in one piece. We had narrowly escaped a gang of would-be counterfeit bag thieves, and we had managed to evade the Wolfe Pack and a crazed horde of irate fashion aficionados thanks to Mr. CEO, Eduard August-Reynard (fondly referred to as ER) and his various forms of transportation— namely a golf cart, a '51 Bentley Mark VI, and a jet black

175

Versace-appointed Bell Textron 430 private helicopter (our personal fave) that whisked us to de Gaulle Airport. (Needless to say, the peerless ER is now officially Caprice's love interest.)

Anyway, back in Paris things had gone from moderately chaotic to completely insane. For one thing, it turned out that after I'd IM-ed Evie re: Leslie sighting on the train, she and her *nouveau* boyfriend, Gerard, had moved some of our stuff, along with the collection, to her parents' suite at the Plaza Athénée in hopes of avoiding any further contact with Leslie—a prudent move, given the circumstances. And another thing—the weirdest thing of all—I received an IM from Priscilla, asking me to meet her for lunch. Oddly enough, she'd been in Paris for a week and had apparently left numerous messages for me at Chez Mwah.

I mean, I'm not the type of person to hold a grudge, and far be it from me to act rudely. So I came to the conclusion that the best way to dignify her invitation would be to give her a true sense of the native customs of France: Ignore!

Since Monsieur X was now a confirmed UFO (unidentified fashion oracle), Mercie went into overdrive, modifying the official press release to include new, highly dubious information about his Zoroastrian monk status, which, according to her, strictly forbade his ego to participate in any form of adoration—public or otherwise—so it was unlikely he would be present at the unveiling of his own brilliant collection.

Another teeny problem was the never-ending model strike, now hung up on biodegradable hair spray and celebrity chef lunches. With Caprice having flown off into the sunset with

ER (who could blame her), and with no resolution in sight, we decided on a bold move — actually, it was the *only* move left: recruit models from the crowds of Japanese tourists that flocked to Louis Vuitton. I know it sounds completely crazy, but, as they say, desperate times call for desperate measures. Anyway, we lucked out, recruiting a group who turned out to be a women's basketball team, known in semi-professional athletic circles as the Hatsuhana Hurricanes.

Mercie then proceeded to spin the whole thing into a "style innovation" story without anyone ever questioning its sheer outré-ness kind of "The Emperor's New Clothes" in reverse.

All of this would have been just fine except that the Hurricanes fell under the impression they were contestants on a reality television show aptly entitled *X*. How they came up with the idea was simply beyond us but, not wanting to risk losing them, Mercie made a big deal of introducing Mick as one of the show's producers — an idea he seemed to enjoy enormously.

A bit later that night (T minus thirty hours until the show), I arrived at the houseboat. Everything was in full swing, as if it were midafternoon. News trucks were already filling up Avenue de Suffren in anticipation of the big event, while swarms of carpenters, electricians, movers, decorators, security guards, and a small team of PR interns were shouting frantic, last-minute instructions. Having overcome most of the major stumbling blocks leading up to the event, my life had now become a series of "what ifs"—what if the models stumbled on the runway; what if Spring's deal didn't happen; what if a meteorite fell from the sky and destroyed the houseboat.

Mercie and Spring had decided to use the dock that ran between Hautelaw and M. Dumfries's boat next door as the runway, with the quai, the walkway along the river, as the staging area. The production crew, hired by Mercie, set up chic white tents for dressing, staging, and press conferences. A huge white scrim with a luxurious silver X pattern had been placed in front of the tents to hide them from the audience and make a chic complement to the enormous shimmering X Mercie had had erected at the river end of the runway.

In addition, Dax had done exactly what he set out to do: transform Spring's old houseboat into an architectural showpiece. It was like a floating version of the Guggenheim at Bilbao meets the Sydney Opera House. Sweeping pearl white forms and sensual angles evoked a sleek, airy feeling of continuous flight.

I made my way across the dock. Electricians were busy draping an enormous web of transparent wiring across rows of high aluminum posts lining both sides of the dock. Suspended in the wiring were hundreds of tiny halogen pin lights that would illuminate the runway like brilliant stars in the night sky. At the far end, I spotted Dax leading a small coterie of carpenters onto M. Dumfries's boat. I lingered briefly, contemplating his good looks. Then I ducked inside.

"Hi, come on in and grab a seat," Mercie said, sitting beside a desk full of reams of lists, files, and newspaper clippings. A small office in back of the mobile atelier (aka tent) housed Mercie. She and an intern were huddled around a PowerBook, a couple of BlackBerrys, and a half dozen cell phones. "You're just in time."

"For what?"

"My tip sheet's just about to be e-mailed to the press. Here," she said, handing me a BlackBerry.

What: Monsieur X Debut Collection Launch

Who: Hosted by Hautelaw Paris

When: 20 July

Where: Houseboat on the Seine

Wear: Monsieur X No. 5 (clothing optional)

"Nice," I said, returning to her BlackBerry.

In reality it made me queasy. Along with everything else that was going on. I braced myself at every new turn for disaster.

"By the way, I heard you met my boss," Mercie said.

"I did?"

"She was one of those people you left behind at Hotel du Cap-Ferrat. I believe you stole her hat."

"Ohmigod, that was her? I'm sooo sorry! Does she know it was me?" Oh, great. She already thinks I'm a thief. Just another one of many who are in for the biggest disappointment of their lives.

"Let's just say all is forgiven. After all, she was beyond ecstatic that the world's most sought-after designer is our newest client, is he not? In fact, I'll be made a partner after all is said and done."

Mercie seemed to have everything under control. Her natural good nature allowed her to remain unfazed by the pressure. Evie, on the other hand, was beginning to show some signs of strain. It was time for the final run-through.

I slipped into the other tent, where a few last-minute fittings were taking place and stylists were matching the bags, shoes, and hose up with the models. Mick and Malcolm stood calmly in the middle of the runway looking over a clipboard.

"Next!" Mick shouted to the stand-in models.

"I'll go next," I said, stepping in front of him.

"There you are!" He grinned, giving me a big hug. "I thought you were tied up with Spring."

"How goes the hunt?" Malcolm said jokingly.

I wanted to confide in Mick and Malcolm, but I couldn't. I didn't think they'd be particularly sympathetic to the truth, with so much of their time spent on this event. So I just smiled and pretended everything was fine.

We all worked feverishly into the night wrapping up the last of the details. The seamstresses were buzzing like a hive of bees on last-minute alterations—their sewing machines whirred feverishly, while Evie and another woman, presumably her head seamstress, were pinning embroideries, flowers, and other embellishments around the hems and skirts of the gowns. After a full rehearsal, with lights, models, hair, and makeup tests, and of course, the clothes, we were finally on the last legs of a long and trying journey. In less than twenty-four hours, we would know our fate. Monsieur X's debut collection would either be a smashing success or a complete flop.

Everyone yawned their *au revoirs*, leaving Dax and me to close up.

Dax was standing on a very tall ladder in the main room, presumably making a few final fixes. He asked me to hold the ladder in place while he reached up to screw in the last two bulbs. I held the ladder, as he'd asked, while Dax reached up to fit the last lightbulb in the low-hanging chandelier.

"Can you hand me the screw, *chérie*?"

How could I say no? I climbed up the ladder and just as the screw in my upstretched fingers reached his, a song floated out of Dax's boom box (note: It was a really sad love song). A tear rolled down my cheek and I began sneezing. Which happens only when I cry, and only when I'm in France. Although it's been over a month, I was still a complete basket case when I heard sad love songs. The Paolo Pangs were just as strong.

I was on the second-to-top-rung of the ladder, when suddenly I lost my balance and grabbed at anything to prevent myself from falling backward. I spotted the bandanna peeking out of Dax's back pocket. I overreached, grabbing on to his shorts instead. By then I was in free fall, sliding all the way down the ladder—shorts in hand, leaving him in nothing more than a pair of Tin Tin boxer shorts! It would have been adorable were it not so firsthand embarrassing!!

181

Dax laughed. I immediately turned a bright crimson and looked away. There in the doorway stood Paolo.

My heart leaped into spasms. "PAOLO!! What are you doing here?"

In the blink of an eye, his expression went from joy to anger. He turned to leave.

"Wait, Paolo. It's not what you think! I was just trying to grab onto something."

"Yes, and I see you found it!" Paolo replied angrily.

Depression. Anger. Codependency. Jealousy. Addiction. Impatience. What do all these things have in common? To the French, they're all manifestations of love.

For the past two hours, I've had an uncontrollable case of the weepies—a disease strictly reserved for girls. Boys are completely immune. With the exception of Toy, who sat steadfastly at my side, whimpering.

As it is my sworn duty to record the events of my life for future posterity, I shall persevere with this journal notation in the hopes that the following incidents might benefit, in some small way, girls such as I, who brave the harsh and treacherous road that leads to their true calling in life—even if it is complete and utter ruin. Please bear with me as I fight back tears while devouring a quart of dulce de leche ice cream. As for tomorrow? With any luck, I'll be in a deep and semi comatose sleep the entire day—if not from a complete nervous breakdown, then from a massive sugar overdose.

Mental note: Check out plot availability at Père Lachaise Cemetery.

As I was about to pass out, I caught a glimpse of myself as I licked the last drop off the gleamy Puiforcat silver spoon.

Oh, great—a pimple!

A cork popped and I spun around. Dax ambled slowly toward me, his dark silhouette muscular and sultry. A bottle of something looking very bubbly dangled from one hand. Two glistening flutes dangled from the other. Everything seemed so beautiful, like a soft dream that had always been present but would only reveal itself when the time was right; the kind of enchantment that needed perfection of time and place to release its hypnotic spell. I closed my eyes in the hopes of capturing this special moment. I also closed them to block out the memory of Paolo's face when he saw me on the ladder with Dax.

When I opened my eyes, I was standing on the most quintessentially romantic French balcony off Dax's tiny jewel box of an apartment. Though the apartment was small, the balcony was amazing. It opened onto the lower mansard rooftop, which peeked out from atop his building. It was the perfect moment, I thought, gazing out across the city bathed in a shimmering golden glow. From this one little peak, all of Paris stretched below.

After Paolo's unexpected and ill-timed entrance, and quick exit, all I wanted to do was go home to Chez Mwah. But with Leslie's unknown status and turmoil everywhere, I wasn't sure what to do or where to go. This was one time I didn't want to be with Evie, either. I didn't want to hear what a rat Paolo was. And I didn't want to wallow in my weepies any longer. I wanted to feel something beside Paolo Pangs, guilt, and self-loathing. I wanted to feel loved.

A crescent moon slung across a velvet sky of summer stars, shimmering from heat that gently rose above the sleeping Earth. I stood there for a long time, not thinking, not feeling, just being, until a warm breeze brought me back and I realized Dax was gone.

I went inside, following the dusky smell of roses and the trail of silky pink petals that led into his bedroom.

He leaned over me, brushing his lips against mine. The heat poured off his smooth, muscular body. "You smell beautiful," he said. It didn't help my conscience that I was wearing my latest scent re-infatuation, "My Sin." He pulled me close, and we fell into a deep, long kiss.

His scent and the way he felt when we kissed . . . it all began to have a weird power over me and I didn't want to rein it in anymore. I wanted to just give in to *l'amour*. . . .

Dax dimmed the lights, poured, and far away, faint sounds of music floated on the air. He kissed me again, and the world had an unreal quality to it and I felt as if I were dreaming.

The candles grew low and flickered and I fell, gently, deeply, into the sweet dream of desire. We kissed again and a world of rose petals engulfed me.

chapter fourteen

Premature Deject-ulation!

date: JULY 20
mood: LOST AND CONFUSED

✳ ✳ ✳

heard music playing somewhere far, far away. It was one of my favorite songs. In fact, I liked it so much that I'd made it my ring tone. The song played again until finally the proverbial lightbulb went on. It's my phone! I thrust a hand out and groped blindly for my bag. But just as suddenly as it began, the ring tone ceased. I groaned and unsuccessfully attempted to lick my lips. My mouth was completely parched— apparently, apart from my hair, which was matted and damp and stuck to my sweaty cheek, there was no moisture left in my entire body. Residual makeup was seemingly caked to my eyelids, making them difficult to open; the smoky blue smear on my pillow was evidence of that. I groped for my sunglasses. Where was I? A momentary bout of amnesia floated above my consciousness. The ring tone again. This time I managed to locate its source.

"Hello?" I rasped.

"Where are you? Do you know what time it is?" Evie snapped.

I jerked the phone away from my head.

"Imogene! Imogene! Answer me!"

I placed the phone on the floor, muffling Evie's agitated voice, and scanned my unfamiliar environment. Withered rose petals were strewn hither and yon—across a plush taupe carpet, in my hair, and stuck tattoo-style, to my legs, arms, and dress.

"OHMIGOD!!" A BFO (blinding flash of obvious!) hit me. I bolted upright. "I'm in Dax's apartment!! Toy!" I whispered. He was sitting in the bedroom doorway facing the open door. "Come here." I knew what he was up to—he was channeling guard dog. "Come on," I urged, "we've got to go." He trotted over reluctantly, for once in his life obeying me.

No sooner had I stood up when my back began to spasm wildly—no doubt from sleeping on a sofa half my size all night. I yelped in pain, which frightened Toy, which made him bark, which destroyed my last shot nerve, causing me to shriek at the top of my lungs when the memory of last night returned.

The sound of my own voice startled me. It rumbled through my head like a thunderstorm.

"Imogene!!" Evie hollered through the phone.

I strained my brain to piece together last night's scenario. What happened?

"Imogene!!" Evie yelled again, louder than ever. "Pick up the phone!" I did, for fear she'd freak out and do something like call the police, or my parents, or the Foreign Legion.

"Hi . . ."

"Where are you? I've been looking everywhere for you. Are you okay?" There was so much background noise that it was hard to understand her. It sounded as if she were standing in the middle of the Macy's Thanksgiving Day Parade.

"I'm okay. I'm with . . . Dax . . . I mean, I'm at his apartment . . . I think."

"Think?" she sputtered, "You *think* you're at his apartment? Listen to me, girlene, aside from everything else, which I won't go into now, if you were in fact thinking, you'd know that your *new* boyfriend is just a knockoff of your old boyfriend! Counterfeit, just like those bags."

"Haven't you heard?" I sniffled sadly. "Fake is the new real . . ."

"Look, I'm sure Dax is a really great guy. I like him a lot. But I think you're confusing infatuation with something more. Admit it."

"Okay, I admit it. I'm infatuated. I have been known to do that on occasion." It's one of my minor talents. I can also cross my eyes. "And what's the difference, anyway?"

"The difference is that you and Paolo are not over. But you already know that."

"Do I? Then how could he let me go off to Paris without a word? What did he think would happen to 'us'?" I had her there.

"The real question is what did *you* think would happen? Now don't say another word, just listen. Priscilla was here early this morning. She has been trying to see you. It turns out that Paolo gave her something to bring you, since she was coming to France on holiday. But when she couldn't reach you, she began to worry, so she called Paolo."

"What are you talking about?"

"I'm talking about the fact that you've got unfinished business with Paolo. I won't be judgmental about whatever you and Dax did last night. But, look, whatever it is, it's not fair. Not to Dax, not to Paolo—and most important, not to you."

OMG! BFO II! All this time I'd been angry with Paolo, when I was really angry with myself. Not because I felt abandoned by him, which I thought I had, but because I'd lost my sense of independence—my ability to be *moi*. It also dawned on me that Paolo must have sensed it as well.

"What would I do without you, Evie?" I said.

"No idea. Just haul your ass out of there—NOW—and get down to the show, Q.F.H.!!"

"Ohmigod, the show!" I shrieked. "I'll be right there!" I hoped to sneak out and explain things later when I actually knew what I was supposed to be explaining. I slipped on my left shoe but couldn't find my right.

"Toy, go find my shoe. Go on, boy," I whispered. His little ears perked up and he dutifully ran into the other room. Unfortunately, he returned with not only my shoe, but with a sleepy Dax, as well.

"Oh. I, uh . . . I . . . we didn't mean to wake you."

"Is everything all right?"

"No. I mean, yes. I mean, I don't know. Look, whatever happened last night . . ."

"You fell asleep in the middle of a kiss. Not that my kisses are all that spectacular . . ."

"They are," I whispered.

"Thank you. And I like to think they don't make people drowsy."

I just stared at him blankly. As if to say, *What happened?*

"You fell asleep . . . and began snoring."

"I don't snore."

"It's cute in a noisy sort of way . . . unless you're a light sleeper. Which I am."

"But did I . . . did we . . . " I couldn't even manage to say the words of what I feared might have happened between us.

"Don't worry. Nothing happened," he said.

I sat back down with a sigh of relief, Toy and shoe plopped into my lap.

Dax sat down next to me. "You also talk," he added.

"I don't."

"You do. About Paolo."

"Paolo!"

"This Paolo . . . you're in love with him still? That's what you said last night . . . in your sleep."

189

"I . . . I didn't think I was. I mean, we're not together any-more."

"You should have told me that you still had feelings for someone else."

All at once I felt a stab of guilt. I really, really liked Dax. But I guess I really still loved Paolo. "I didn't know."

"How could you not know what is in your heart?"

Okay, that was the sixty-four-thousand-dollar question. How could I *not* have known? How could I have spent an entire summer away from the one person on earth that I cared about more than anyone else? An unanticipated tear sprung forth.

"I'm so sorry, Dax," I sobbed. "I honestly didn't know. I didn't mean to hurt you."

"I know that." He smiled.

"I *never* meant to hide anything from you," I blubbered on.

Dax took my hand and said, "Sometimes what is right in front of us is hardest to see."

Did I mention French is the language of philosophy? Anyway, Dax, as always, was wonderful, which made it all the more painful. And I think both of us realized that in a different time and place this would have been a romance . . . maybe even a great one. But I already had a great romance—or at least I once did.

chapter fifteen

Pret-a-Partay

date: JULY 20

mood: LIGHTS! CAMERAS!
LIP GLOSS!

While some travel to Disneyland to be amused, with each new season the fashion flock heads off for their own brand of entertainment: the fashion show.

✳   ✳   ✳

I hit the ground running, making it to the Plaza Athénée suite, where I showered (Toy too!), gulped down a couple of aspirin, dressed, grabbed my camcorder and the daily *MMD*, and shot out the door in record time, wet hair and all.

My head was still pounding something fierce. And my stomach was twisted beyond a Gordian knot over my ruined love life. But because I had to be completely together when I got to the show, I vowed to fall apart later.

I checked my watch. It was five o'clock. I was good, already making great time.

When I rounded the corner, the top of the houseboat came into view. The smell of flowers and the surrounding trees' little pink and white blossoms falling like snow all around added to the wonderland. The once total dump had gone glam. It was stunning.

I stopped at the edge of the crowd. You could feel the excitement. It was the Oscars of fashion. I'm not going to go into the long list of socialites, celebrities, and distinguished persons who flowed past Toy *et moi*—it was an endless river of glittering stars. And the atmosphere was charged with a zillion sparking electrons.

When I reached the houseboat, harried and out of breath, I was shocked to find Caprice standing by a doorway.

"Ohmigod! What are you doing out here?!" I wheezed, placing Toy on the ground and taking my camcorder out of my bag.

"Waiting for you. I was beginning to think you weren't coming," she said, chuckling. "Been swimming?"

"I'm so behind schedule," I heaved, pushing damp hair out of my eyes. "What are *you* doing here? I figured you'd be skiing in the Andes with ER by now."

"Are you kidding? I wouldn't miss this for the world! Besides, who's going to model the clothes?" She put her hand up. "Don't answer that, I've met the ball team."

"You know, they're not half bad. . . ."

"They're fabulous! But I brought some friends along, just in case."

As she turned to walk away, I asked, "Hey! What happened with the strike?"

"Simply a matter of social pressure—something you can thank Olivier DeDompierre for."

"O.D.D.?"

"Yup. Once he made it known that there were no seats left, widespread panic took over. And since anybody who was anybody couldn't possibly miss out on what promised to be the show of the millennium, it was simply a matter of pointing out to the union that the only way they were going to be *at* the show was to be *in* the show. And to be *in* the show, the strike had to be settled."

"What about your demands?"

"With the exception of Latvian massage therapists, we got what we wanted." She winked and slipped through the door.

I took a minute, then followed her inside. Naturally it was complete bedlam. Hatsuhana Hurricanes mingled among supermodels, and makeup artists rushed through the backstage tent—our mobile atelier.

I spotted my target: Evie. She was surrounded by her army of seamstresses and in the center of it all, madly rushing from model to model, addressing any necessary last-minute alterations.

I raced over to where she was standing and spun her around to face me. I saw it coming a mile away, though I should mention the warning signs weren't exactly subtle. I mean, as soon as Evie looked at me she assumed her classic "prepare to be lectured" stance—hands on hips, eyes narrowed, lips pursed. She was ready to unload her entire seventeen years of life experience condensed into a single semierratic burst onto yours truly.

I should point out that said reprimand wasn't about being late for the biggest event of our lives. I mean, on any other planet, that *alone* would be reason enough for justifiable homicide, right? But not on planet Evie. Because on planet Evie things like global chaos, killer asteroids, or the end of the universe as we know it took a backseat to her personal relationships—especially when those personal relationships involved doing stupid things that put their (and her) future happiness in jeopardy.

"Wait." I held up my hand, hoping to head her off at the pass. "Before you start, I just want to say you were right. I mean, about the 'we vortex' and everything."

Evie relaxed her shoulders and exhaled. "I'm listening."

"I mean, even though Dax is wonderful, and is everything a girl like *moi* could ever ask for, I realize I could never be happy with him . . . or with Paolo, or anyone else for that matter, because my happiness can only come from inside of me, not outside."

Evie slowly nodded her head, her pursed lips easing into a wry, knowing smile. You know, the kind of smile that only someone who knows you all too well, but who still cares deeply about you in spite of yourself, can manage.

"You've done well, grasshopper."

Well, it turned out that the Tiffany's box that Saffron saw Paolo giving to Priscilla that day on Greenwich Avenue was not for Priscilla, but for me.

"Somehow it came to Paolo's attention that Priscilla was

going to Paris with her family for summer vacation. She was just the messenger, that's all," Evie said.

I was in a state of shock. "How do you know that? Where is he now? Did Paolo tell you that?"

"No. Priscilla did. She's out there," Evie told me. "I gave her a front-row seat. After all, it's the least I could do. I'm really sorry, Im." She put her arms around me. "I messed up. It's my fault that I let hearsay cause all these problems."

Just then, Evie's head seamstress interrupted us.

"One minute," Evie replied. Then she turned to me and said, "I've been putting out fires all day."

"Evie . . . wait," I said, wanting to know more. "Where's Paolo?" But she was already sprinting across the floor to her waiting seamstress.

I stood there holding Toy. In the middle of a cyclone a voice said, "Oh look, Minty! It's, like, that secrets girl."

It was Ferebee. And Minty.

"Oh, right." Minty waved. "Hey, what network does the Monsieur X show air on?"

"Yeah!" Ferebee added. "Like, what's the prize?"

Several of the Hurricanes had gathered around and were giggling. Apparently they'd had been talking up the reality show and were getting anxious.

"You know," I said, "you'll have to ask the producer about that."

The Hurricanes shouted "Mick!" in unison and began glancing around furtively. I felt bad for Mick.

"This is a reality show?" asked Caprice.

"Don't ask," I muttered, pulling her away from the group.

Needless to say, with the real models now officially in the show, as well as the Japanese tourists, and the Hurricanes, there was a lot of refitting and last-minute adjustments to be made. I dove in and spent the next hour in an anxious flux, running around like a maniac helping Evie and Mercie, and fielding several hundred phone calls from a very nervous Spring. Miraculously, I managed to pry my way into one of the chairs for an exclusive (and desperately needed) hair and makeup creation by the one and only Angelique, *coiffeuse* to the rich, the famous, and the occasional aspiring intern.

By sundown we were as ready as we were ever going to be. "No pressure," I murmured to myself as I climbed to the top of the stairs and took my position at the gate next to Mercie. Already the red carpet was lined with paparazzi, checking equipment and eagerly chatting amongst themselves while security paced back and forth, looking expectantly terse.

A slight breeze had picked up, carrying with it the faint smell of jasmine flowers and the sounds of the jazz quartet tuning up on deck. I looked back one last time, at the sleek and delicate canopy that traversed the two houseboats. Its fabric was elegantly folded in arches, forming a tunnel of light and ending in a great, shimmering X. The clear purple of a late afternoon sky and the dark waters of the Seine flowing beyond were rich and lustrous. I turned and looked at Mercie.

"Ready?" I giggled nervously, quelling

the bevy of butterflies that had suddenly taken flight in my stomach. Mercie exhaled slowly and squeezed my hand. "Ready, *pardner*."

Naturally, Spring timed her arrival perfectly, her Mercedes pulling in between a famous rock star and the current French ambassador to the United States and distinguished personage about town. Scurrying around to the back car door, her driver opened it and Spring (along with a small group of retail executives) made her move out of the car in a puff of coral and white, lighter-than-air chiffon. Her two dogs tumbled out as a second lean leg and a Louboutin-adorned foot hit the ground. To accessorize, she was wearing a gorgeous cabochon coral bead necklace, with beads the size of meteorites. Tonight Spring would define chic.

"It's a tad warm for leather today, isn't it, dear?" she cooed to the rock legend.

"I'm rock," he said firmly before scurrying away, "I do leather."

Spring proceeded to lead her powerful little coterie of Big Apple buyers to the gate as the strobes began popping. Her famous pearly whites, or I should say, blinding whites came out on cue to perform their glistening duty. I was in the middle of calculating the possible cost per incisor when, after a brief, and no doubt tactical, exchange of pleasantries with Charles Rochefort III, she spotted Mercie and me.

"Imogene! Mercie! DAAAAAAAHLINGS!!" she cried, waving a matching coral print clutch at us. This was followed by a series of air kisses and a covert "Are we good to go?" whispered into my ear.

"We're good." I smiled reassuringly.

"Fabu," she said, smiling at us both. "I'll meet you inside." And with that, she turned her veneers back toward the strobes like a moth to the flame. Supermodel instincts die hard.

I squeezed my way past a gaggle of Grandes Dames, practically fainting from the effects of secondhand perfume. For one déjà vu moment I thought I was on back the main floor of Bloomingdale's. I moved inside, where social jockeying had reached unheard-of heights as a *Diorgy* of chicsters air kissed flocks of Lacroixific trendsters to within an inch of their lives. Arab princes and princesses collided with supersocialettes, who collided with the crème brûlée of the art world. There were media barons, financial world tycoons, celebrities, fashion fiends, rock stars; you name it, they were all there.

The room was filled with beautiful people celebrating their fabulous genes (not to mention their fabulous jeans—did I mention denim is back?). With nary a stand-in sight. Okay, pulling it all together had been somewhat of a challenge for us. But if there's one thing you can say about us, it's that we're always up for a challenge. And I guess our plan was working because our fashion event, judging by the volume of media swirling around the models, was a huge success.

I spotted Dax, squeezing his way through the next room, and apparently Mercie did too.

"Oh, there's Dax," she said, half-surprised. She looked at me sideways, thinking out loud. "Are you two still . . ."

"Go for it," I said, giving her a gentle nudge, which was

all it took. Before I could laud Dax and all his attributes, she was off after him. Actually, I think they just might make a wonderful couple.

I wondered where Paolo was and searched the rows of seats. I spotted Priscilla in her front-row seat, just as Evie had said. I felt terrible for believing Saffron's e-mail. I've always liked Priscilla. I was glad she was here and made a promise to myself to say so after the show.

Slowly the lights began to dim, leaving an expectant hush that blanketed the atmosphere. A pounding bass line shattered the silence as the runway lit up like a supernova. I slipped into my reserved seat next to the runway, pulled the lens cap off my camcorder, and hit record. The sound was on, the lighting was good, Toy was sitting on my lap on his best behavior, and my outfit rocked!

All heads turned as Caprice rounded the screen and strutted down the runway in perfect form—confident, elegant, and most of all, *deadly chic*. A jeweled bag finished her outfit, and the effect was *devastating*! I mean, it was one thing to see the collection in a fitting room, or paraded around a hotel hallway, but here, under the brilliant lights, with all of Paris holding their collective breath, it seemed as if the past had somehow returned.

An eerie tension hushed the crowd—not a cough, not a whisper, not a single strobe went off; only the rhythmic thump of woofers as Caprice turned at the giant *X*, tilted her hips, and headed back up the runway.

I managed to steal a glance at Spring, seated on the top deck of HLP, for her reaction. She was carefully eyeing the audience, madly chain-smoking while eagerly waiting for a response, any response. As Caprice neared the end of the runway, Kimi appeared from behind the screen, rolling her hips like a pro. The tension broke in a shock wave of applause, the audience roared their approval. The girls did a low five as they passed each other. Kimi strutted smooth and easy, spinning neatly at the X and walking back with the brashness of a superstar. If this really *were* a reality show, she would have won hands down.

And so the evening went, model after model, outfit after outfit, each more gorgeous than the last. Dresses had a vintage Hollywood feel from the forties. With Evie's touches however, the resulting look was beyond modern.

Evie had known exactly what to do, color-coding the entire collection for maximum impact. Her reds alone were dazzling: Claret, Carnation, Crimson, Cerise, Flame, Port, Ruby, Garnet, Scarlet, Vermillion, and Terra-Cotta draped and sewn in every fabric from shimmering chiffons to satin velvets, and of course, the fabulous jeweled bags. And speaking of bags, Mercie had created goodie bags with all the gifts I had received the last few weeks from would-be patrons, and regifted them as swag bags at the fashion show. As far as I could tell, nobody recognized any of it.

At long last the greatly anticipated finale—when all the girls came out for one last look and the designer received his well-deserved kudos, was about to begin. For our part, Spring, knowing there would be no Monsieur X in attendance, insisted she appear on his behalf, taking bows and making a few well-placed remarks about his self-effacing spiritual dogma. And I, as his sole confidante, was to walk out onstage when she finished to convey his personal thanks and best wishes to his adoring audience.

Unfortunately, as I stood poised to go out on the runway, a voice from deep within my soul screamed, YOU ARE A LIAR, IMOGENE! A BIG FAT LIAR! Talk about bad timing, I mean, I realized at that point that I just couldn't go through with the hoax any longer. I knew I had to go out there alone on that runway and tell the truth. Just me, myself, and *moi*.

Okay, so maybe this wasn't the best time for revelations of this sort, especially ones that involved the reigning crème de la crème of society, several hundred thousand dollars, and countless people's hopes and dreams for a better life. But deep down I knew that in spite of everything, I had to tell the truth. I mean, who was going to speak out on behalf of the brilliant designer whose work was now the toast of Paris? Whose work *I* had exploited to keep my job in Paris? The obvious answer was simple: Go out on stage and announce that there was no Monsieur X; that I had perpetrated a hoax upon an innocent (not quite) and well-meaning (not entirely) public, and that I, and I alone, was *solely responsible* for the repercussions of these actions.

Then a thought came to me and gave me the courage and reassurance to prevail over my otherwise desperate uncertainty. And it didn't come in the form of a character I was channeling, or a tiny angel on my shoulder, either, but in the form of a real one, of a love deemed lost and found again, one that I had prayed would return to me.

I was standing next to Spring as the last of the girls filed out on stage. She puffed furiously at a cigarette, watching her dogs tug on their coral-encrusted leashes, anxious to get to the runway and wreak doggie havoc on the unsuspecting models. Then suddenly, for some cosmic reason, Spring turned to me and smiled tenderly.

"I want you to know, Imogene," she said quickly, her voice husky, emotional, "that I'll never forget this evening as long as I live. And you, my dear, made it happen."

And with that she was gone, heading down the runway into a maelstrom of strobe lights like it was 1985 all over again. The audience leapt to its feet, cheering and clapping for all they were worth; and Spring, with all her good-natured craziness, was the "It Girl" once more.

chapter sixteen

Get Your Rocks Off!

date: JULY 20
(AKA, A MOMENT LATER)
mood: FLABBERGASTED!

❄   ❄   ❄

You've done a wonderful job with the show," a familiar voice behind me said. I went rigid for a second, refusing to believe my ears, fearing it might have been my overtaxed imagination. Then a hand touched my shoulder and as always, whenever he touched me, my body quaked. I felt a tremendous burst of energy, like I might turn to mush and have a nervous breakdown all at the same time. He gently turned me around and we stood there for a long time, looking into each other's eyes, barely breathing.

We blurted out in unison: "I'm sorry."

"No, it was my fault," Paolo said softly. "I shouldn't have jumped to conclusions. I should have trusted you."

"I'm the one who should have trusted."

"I missed you," he said, as my heart practically pounded out of my chest. He handed me a blue box with a white satin ribbon. I untied the perfect bow and slowly lifted the lid. But before I peered inside, I said, "But why were you so eager for me to go to Paris for the summer in the first place?"

"I wasn't. I bit my tongue, fearing I'd hold you back. I knew it would be a great experience for you. Even if it meant I'd be spending all summer without you. And missing you every minute. I knew you wouldn't go if I asked you not to. And I didn't want to stand in your way."

Très melt!

"Aren't you going to open it?" he said.

I lifted the top off, and there were the most perfect, the most dazzling, heart-shaped aquamarine earrings.

"Paolo!" I cried, hugging him like mad.

We laughed and kissed, and for the first time all summer I felt as if all were right with the world again. Well, almost.

"Hey, girlene!" Evie shouted, hurrying toward us. She eyed Paolo and grinned. "Welcome back, stranger. Listen, I hate to bother you at a time like this, but isn't that your cue?"

Evie pointed a finger toward Spring, who was standing in the middle of the runway. Spring smiled at the crowd, glanced furtively in my direction, and spoke into the microphone.

"As I was saying . . . and Monsieur X's confidante and muse, Hautelaw's own Imogene!"

"Ohmigod! I have to go!" I turned to leave but spun back, looking Paolo straight in the eyes. "Don't you dare move a muscle!"

Evie looped her elbow in his and squeezed. "Don't worry. I'll keep an eye on him."

I turned my attention toward the runway.

"You can do this," I repeated to myself as I sped out onto the runway before the cheering crowd. I should tell you, I had absolutely no idea what I was going to say when I got out there.

Spring winked and handed me the mic. I looked into the audience, took a deep breath, and plunged in.

"Thank you all for coming this evening. I'm sure the designer would be very honored by your kindness and enthusiasm."

The audience responded with a burst of applause and shouts of "Tell us who he is!" and "When is he coming?"

"Well," I soldiered on, "that's exactly what I'm here to tell you. I'm here to tell you that Monsieur X . . ."

A gasp ripped through the crowd as all heads turned. I spun around and there was Georges, casually walking up the runway. He looked ten years younger; his hair was no longer white, but a soft brown. It was pulled back into a ponytail, and he was very tan. But there was something else different about him. He reeked cool. From his mirror-tinted shades to his stiff, high-collared black ruffled shirt, military jacket, gold-chain-draped fingerless leather gloves, skinny black jeans, and shiny black boots. *Très Marquis de Mode!*

A curious smile played on his lips as he scanned the audience through his sunglasses, slowly drinking in their astonished faces and fervent whispers of disbelief.

"Mademoiselles," he said lightly, taking his place between us as if he really belonged there.

"I'm sorry," Spring sputtered, clearly puzzled, "I don't believe we've met. Though you do look faintly familiar."

"Oh, Spring," I said as casually as I could muster, "this is Georges. My aunt's concierge."

"Your aunt's concierge?" she repeated, eyeing him carefully. "I seeeeee."

While she was busy trying to understand what that could possibly have to do with anything, I turned to Georges and whispered frantically, "This is very sweet of you, Georges, but you don't have to do this. I've decided to tell the truth!"

"Ah, Mademoiselle Imogene, that is precisely why I am here."

"I don't understand," I stammered.

"Neither do I," Spring said, intrigued.

Georges nodded to her and smiled cordially. "It is very simple Mademoiselle Spring Sommer. I am, as you say, Monsieur X."

"You?!"

"It is true. But you will probably know me by the name I used in my previous life," he said passionately, turning to the audience with his arms out as if to embrace them, *"Yves Montrachet!"*

"What?" I said, stunned. "But why?"

"Because, *chérie*, dresses were the tragedy of my life! But you've cured me. I'm a new man." Then he winked at me.

The crowd leaped to their feet in a fit of ecstasy, reeling with joy at the return of the great French designer. A meteoric rise from nowhere to fashion glory—there's nothing fashion loves more than a comeback story.

Spring, no fool, pounced on him, threading her elbow through his, in hopes of preventing escape.

Yves Montrachet, as it turned out, wasn't dead after all. Nor was he in the designer relocation program. No, he was living right here under our upturned noses the whole time. Though how he ever managed to stay incognito is still a head scratcher. (I told you concierges were magicians!) Having dropped the A-bomb of the fashion millennium in the middle of everything, Georges, or Monsieur X, or Yves Montrachet, or whatever you want to call him, went on to address his adoring fans. He thanked them for their warm reception and told the story of his assumed untimely death, or rather, his lengthy hiatus from the fashion universe.

Apparently, having completed his last collection (the one Evie, Caprice, and I had stumbled upon), he felt certain he had created something ahead of its time. *So far ahead*, in fact, that he would rather remove himself from the public eye than risk losing their approval—something he valued more than life itself.

As to his alleged death, he could only surmise that at the time of his decision he had tossed his favorite dress form off the roof of his studio on Rue Mignon (not Gibraltar) to

207

symbolically end his career. (I mean, it just doesn't get any more French than that!) Afterward, he went underground, taking the job with my aunt and moving everything into the hidden room. Having known the previous owners for many years before their move to Rouen, he knew of its existence.

Okay, so there we were, arm in arm before Yves's legion of cheering admirers. He had pulled Evie on stage, publicly expressing his gratitude for her wonderful imagination and professional restraint in bringing his collection up to date, and thanking Mercie, Caprice, and me for bringing it to light after all these years. I mean, it really was the most perfect storybook ending there ever was.

But if there's one thing I've learned, it's that there is no such thing as perfection. Meaning that right in the middle of this flawless fashion fervor, several ushers jumped out on the runway waving guns. Real guns! One of the ushers, who looked suspiciously like Chief Inspector Fitz of the Sûreté in a phony mustache and glasses, stepped forward and shouted, "Everybody freeze!!"

"Funny," Spring said, "that's just what Dr. Schrager says each time he injects the botox."

"I said freeze! And I meant freeze!"

On cue the entire crowd—every licorice stick, socialite, and microdog—registered a pose.

Fitz exhaled loudly and rolled his eyes. "Let me say this another way," he grumbled. "PUT YOUR HANDS IN THE AIR!"

Suddenly it was quieter than the ancient manuscripts room at the Bibliothèque Mazarin.

"Hey, what are *you* doing?" I shouted.

"You *know* this man?!" Spring asked in shock.

"I'm afraid so," I replied indignantly. "He's supposed to be the police."

"And you, *mademoiselle*, are supposed to *fermez la bouche!*"

Fitz, or whoever he was, glared at me, then pointed his chin at Caprice and shouted for his accomplice. "Piggot!"

Piglet appeared from behind a group of Hurricanes, sidled nervously over to Caprice, and yanked a jeweled bag out of her hand.

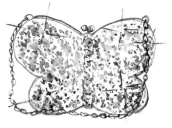

"Hey!" she snapped, slapping his hand away.

Piglet's eyes bulged wildly. He turned and stared hopelessly at Fitz.

"What are you looking at me for, you idiot?" Fitz said. "You have a gun!"

"Excuse me, but what exactly is it you want here?" Spring asked casually.

"It is very simple, *madame*," Fitz said.

"*Mademoiselle*," she corrected.

"Very well, mademoiselle. We wish to take back something that belongs to us."

"You're going to steal our clothes!" Evie gasped.

"*Non*, I am not going to steal your clothes. I am going to steal the bags."

"What do you want those for?" Mercie asked.

"He wants them because they're real," said Leslie, stepping through the crowd. He, along with several other men dressed as caterers and the security officers, walked onto the mobbed runway, pointing their guns at the ushers. It was all very confusing.

"Leslie?" I said, trying to keep my jaw from dropping.

"You know this man too?" asked Spring, even more shocked than before.

"He's my aunt's housekeeper."

"Tamara always was a very unusual person."

"Okay, enough of this," Leslie mumbled. "HANDS UP!!" Needless to say, everyone who was not in possession of a gun raised his or her hands even higher. "I mean the guys with the guns." Leslie sighed.

"What about your guns?" Caprice shouted.

"We're the police. We get guns."

"Ohmigod!" Spring shouted. "There really is a fashion police!"

"You're the police?"

"Customs, actually."

"What did you do with Captain Howdy?!" Evie shouted.

"Who?"

"The stuffed animals we left in the box," I said.

"Oh, them. They're back at headquarters." Leslie snapped his gum and chuckled. "We were going to donate them to the church across the street."

"DON'T YOU DARE!" Evie panicked.

"I thought *they* were the police," I said, keeping my hands in the air and pointing with my chin.

"If they're the police," Leslie said flatly, "why are they pointing guns at you?"

"An excellent question," murmured Yves.

"Well then, who are they?" Evie asked.

"They are diamond smugglers. And this" he said, pointing his gun at Fitz, "is François Fitz Gilbert, one of Europe's most notorious diamond smugglers."

"*Most* notorious," Fitz said with a bow.

"And their vehicles were the bags you found in the Pacojet box. It *was* to be used as part of a sting operation. Unfortunately, you and Miss Thing here"—Leslie cleared his throat loudly and frowned at Evie—"helped yourselves to our bait."

"How did the smugglers know we had them?"

"Excuse me! You were on every newspaper and TV in the country! Fitz and his pals were already watching the house. He recognized his stuff immediately."

"But you followed me on the train."

"I was tailing Fitz, who was after you."

"Ohmigod! We could have been killed!"

"Yeah, well, let that be a lesson to you!"

"Enough of this nonsense," Fitz seethed. "I must ask you, Agent Leslie, to put your gun down!" With that he grabbed Kimi around the neck and waved his gun at her. She winked at me slyly and I panicked, realizing she still thought it was all part of the reality show.

"Kimi, no!!" I hollered.

But it was too late. She spun around in a blur of tae kwon do moves that would have made Jackie Chan envious, sending Fitz flying head over heels into the crowd.

"Ooooooooh!" Evie whispered in awe. "Praying mantis!"

211

As for the rest of the ushers, suffice it to say, it was all over in a matter of minutes. The Hurricanes sprang into action, kicking and punching with the speed and skill of kung fu masters, followed by a stream of gendarmes, who rushed out of the tents and flooded the already overcrowded runway. In their chaotic efforts to apprehend the fleeing jewel thieves, they managed to knock several leading members of polite society, a leather-clad rock star, and Channel 4 news anchor Missy Farthington into the Seine. They also succeeded in arresting O.D.D., who in an unfortunate fit of questionable taste had chosen a red tie and blazer combination that resembled the ushers' uniforms. At some point in the ensuing melee, Paolo appeared with Brooke and Candy Wolfe in tow, dragging them in front of Leslie to report.

"I found these two in the tent. They were stuffing these bags into their bag." Special customs agents, along with officials from the Chambre Syndicale, had to authenticate these designs. "We've been watching you for weeks now, my dear, staking out fakes at the fashion show."

"Take your hands off me, you cretin!" Brooke snarled, looking as though she'd just been dropped in a vat of cake frosting. "Who do you think you're dealing with?"

"That's what we're going to find out, ladies." Leslie grinned.

"Wait a minute! We haven't done anything. It's just a bag!"

"What's the charge?" sneered Candy.

"Try attempted jewel theft on for size."

"Jewels?! What jewels?!!" Brooke sputtered in panic, her eyes suddenly landing on me. "Imogene! We used to work together . . . she'll vouch for me!" She looked at me pleadingly. "Right, sweetie?"

Leslie snapped his gum at me and said, "You know these girls?"

I stared at them for a few seconds, trying to remember, then shook my head innocently. "Never seen 'em."

"She's lying!" Brooke spat.

Leslie waved a couple of gendarmes over. "Take these two away."

can't tell you what a hoot reading the morning papers was the next day. *Le Monde*, *Le Figaro*, the *International Herald Tribune*, and *WWD* all reported the event. The morning was filled with croissants and crèmes and laughs. But we had to see O.D.D.'s column first. And so, with bated breath, we read:

MMD: (PARIS) 21 JULY
ICING ATTACK!
FASHION FORECASTER INVOLVED IN CAKE FIGHT BETWEEN TWO CATWALK CUTIES

Stunner Ferebee, who with BFF Minty was celebrating the end of the model strike, were combatants in a frosty fracas, which erupted after a Wolfe Pack member, who is known only as Brooke, accidentally (or not) smeared icing on her dress while passing through the crowd. It was discovered later that she and her cohorts, Candy Wolfe and Romaine & Fern Snipes, aka

Well, everything got sorted out about Leslie's real identity. I mean, he really *was* a special U.S. Customs agent. And he was staking out the counterfeit-bag-slash-jewel-thieves. One thing that was not a cover was his true love—which really was gastronomy.

While Evie and I were at the hotel, the local baker bought Leslie's croissant recipe, and they've started a franchise together. It's called, aptly enough, The Croissanterie.

Speaking of luck, it turned out that La Lagerfeld himself, the real McCoy, actually attended the show. Mercie, not taking any chances verifying his identity, had immediately ushered him to a front-row seat. Strangely enough, he remembered her (who wouldn't?) and, after pulling off the fête of the century so amazingly, he had no choice but to hire her on the spot as his new PR assistant. I'm keeping my fingers crossed that Mercie will also soon have a new boyfriend in Dax, as well.

Eduard and Caprice were well on their way to a blissfully ever after. After all, he is all about media: film, television, radio, concerts, and publishing. As fate would have it, when Caprice told him about my little memoir project and video diary, he was quite a little bit more than interested.

Spring came through with a check for production, which she presented to Georges-slash-Monsieur X-slash-Yves at the end of the evening, and she promptly reimbursed me for all my expenses. Not only that, but she was beside herself to have started a new trend: houseboats. They've actually become the hottest real estate craze in Paris—everyone's buying them up like mad!

Ferebee and Minty, well, rumor has it that they have been admitted to The Meadows rehab center in Arizona for "work stress image issues."

As for *moi*, I sent Cissy the last of the reimbursements for *Imogenius*. Although it left me broke, I got something back that money can't buy. I got Paris. And as we all know, with Paris comes *l'amour*.

Much later, after the show, Paolo and I found a cozy spot on the top deck of HLP and did some much-needed catching up, if you know what I mean. Evie (who is definitely not a fashion nun anymore) and Gerard danced endlessly into the night, and Mercie—I couldn't help but notice—spent a *lot* of time with Dax (frankly, I think they're completely adorable together). Most of all, though, I watched Yves as he stood happily in the center of it all, surrounded by his old friends and a great many new ones; saying hellos instead of good-byes and promising never, ever, to disappear again.

It was nearly dawn when the last of the cleanup crew mounted the stairs and disappeared into the night. Paolo had stayed behind, helping me put away the last of everything and, in general, was being his old adorable self. (I honestly don't think either of us was about to let the other out of their sight, anyway.)

Eventually, we found ourselves collapsed on deck, nibbling the last of the caterers' tray of petit fours and staring up at the shimmering stars as the last of the radiance from  the City of Light nearly washed away in the early dawn. And the city was ours and ours alone, even if only for this moment.

I drank it in, along with the outline of mysterious little islands on the river and a few shooting stars, which conveniently appeared, heightening the experience manifold. Paolo held up the tie line and put a finger to his lips. He had set us adrift on the Seine, floating endlessly down the river toward a life yet to be revealed and wondrous places of the heart—just the two of us, and petit fours, and Paris eternal.

Heart,

Imogene

Imogene Illuminated

❋ ❋ ❋

Name: Imogene

Age: 17

Status: In a relationship!

Location: Greenwich, CT.

Last Log-in: One-hour ago, pre–35,000 feet above planet Earth

Honors & Awards: The French Legion of Honors (whatever that is)

Occupation: Rising fashion star. (Duh!)

Interests & Hobbies: Finishing my memoirs.

Where I'll Be This Fall: Hint No. 1: Back at GCA for my senior year, working part-time for Hautelaw. Hint No. 2: Insanely in luv!

I Skull & Crossbones: *Imogenius* SoftWear

I Heart: Smart Cars, French BFFs Mercie and Dax, Château de Ver-sigh (a girl can still dream, can't she?), croissants, houseboats, *le coif de* "The Donald," and *l'amour*

Affirmation: *À la phase prochaine!* In other words, on to the next phase! (After all, we'll always have Paris!)